Richard Ball Rutter

Scenes from the Pilgrim's Progress

Richard Ball Rutter

Scenes from the Pilgrim's Progress

ISBN/EAN: 9783337287986

Printed in Europe, USA, Canada, Australia, Japan

Cover: Foto ©Andreas Hilbeck / pixelio.de

More available books at **www.hansebooks.com**

SCENES

FROM THE

Pilgrim's Progress

BY

RICHARD BALL RUTTER

LONDON:

TRÜBNER & Co., LUDGATE HILL

PRINTED BY JOHN BELLOWS, GLOUCESTER

MDCCCLXXXII

Christian and Pliable

"THE Lord Himself will wipe all tears away
    Once and for ever ;" "And with whom shall be
    Our loving converse through that cloudless day?"
Asked Pliable ; said Christian, " We shall see
Seraphs, whose every breath is melody,
Whom but to look on is a dream of joy ;
And, even richer blessing, there shall we
Regain the lost and loved, our first employ
To close the links which death could strain but not destroy.

" Holy and loving, all our sorrows o'er,
Beneath the beam of God's approving eye,
In his known Presence safe for evermore,
How shall we wonder that we feared to die !
There the crowned Elders sit enthroned on high,
There all the pure in heart behold their God ;
Yea death is swallowed up in victory,
For each whose martyred blood cried from the sod,
Shall touch the sceptre there, leaving on earth the rod.

"Some were confumed with fire, fome gave their breath
Up to the cruel fea, for His dear fake
Who gave them ftrength to fight the fear of death ;
And the wild beaft was loofed his prey to make
Of fome whofe dying filence mutely fpake ;
But all are there, they fell afleep in clay,
Enrobed in immortality to wake."
Said Pliable. "While hearing all you fay
Of heavenly joys, the charms of this world melt away."

The Slough of Despond.

. . . . " THE Slough thine eyes furveyed
Cannot be mended, being the defcent
Whereto the bitter tears of hope delayed,
With awful fenfe of former trefpafs blent,
Continually do run, finding no wholefome vent.

" And therefore is the quickfand called Defpond,
For, ever as each confcience wakes from fin,
Doubts, fears, and difmal thoughts, too clofely conned,
Throughout this gloomy fwamp come pouring in,
Efcape from which none without Help can win ;
Such is its caufe, and fo poor fouls are drowned
In its dark quagmires ere they well begin
Their journey, yet the King who owns the ground
Right willingly would make the treacherous footing found.

" His labourers alfo have, under command
Of His furveyors, daily been employed
Thefe fixteen hundred years on this wet land,
Which thus the old high way hath half deftroyed ;
But its ftill hungering maw is never cloyed ;
Though, to my knowledge, there have been," faid he,
" Full twenty thoufand loads fhot down the void,
Yea millions, fo to fpeak, of words which be
Sound as the acorn's firm and time-defying tree,

" And brought throughout the year from every part
Of the King's realms, (and they who know, declare
That if it could be filled by toil or art,
The beſt materials theſe for its repair ;)
But notwithſtanding this His royal care,
'Tis ſtill the ſlough Deſpond, and ſuch for ever,
Though bridged at times by mountain-moving prayer,
Muſt it remain, deſpite all man's endeavour,
For only Help from God paſt guilt from grief can ſever.

" True. 'tis the Law-giver's imperial will
That ſteps of ſtone ſhould croſs the quaking ſlough.
But at ſuch times as it doth overfill
With weeping weather, as it doth e'en now,
What between clouded eye and dizzy brow,
The few who ſee them often ſlip aſide,
And truly, ſink into the mire, as thou
And I can witneſs, yet the ſteps abide ;
But once within the gate, no ſuch falſe ooze ſhall glide."

Worldly Wiseman

ESHREW him for his counfel! well I wot,
My worthy fellow, a more dangerous way
And troublefome, in all the world is not,
Than this one, fhown thee in an evil day,
Which thou fhalt find if thou his rule obey ;
Thou haft, methinks, already tafted forrow,
For I perceive that from Defpond's foul clay
Thou haft been fain a miry cloak to borrow ;
But fmall is this day's grief to that of each to-morrow.

" Hear me who am thy elder, yet again !
Thou art moft fure to meet with, ere the clofe
Of this thy journey, wearinefs and pain,
Hunger and peril, nakednefs and blows,
Wild beafts, and fights more fell than fancy knows,
Horrible darknefs, and to fum up all
Of dreadful in one word, death, far from thofe
Whofe love might turn his arrow in its fall ;
And is not this a fate the boldeft heart to 'appal ?

" Thefe things, my friend, are certain to be true,
Having been proved by many gone before ;
And can fuch blind obedience then be due
To that cold ftranger of thy heart and door ?"
" Why Sir, this burden on my back, is more
Grievous to bear," faid Chriftian, " than the things
Which you have told, ay came they o'er and o'er.
O Sun Divine ! that in her wanderings,
My 'lightened foul might know the healing in Thy wings !"

" Tell me how firft thy heavy burden came ?"
Afked Worldly Wifeman then, and Chriftian faid,
" By reading in this book ;" " I thought the fame,"
Cried the'other, " and, poor pilgrim, thou haft fped
Even as one who rafhly dares to tread
A mifty mountain path at day's decline,
Who falls into an agony of dread
Which fteals his judgment, (as it hath ftolen thine,)
Making the haplefs wretch mad as the thrall of wine."

Evangelist's Second Meeting

"MOVED at the fight, the good Evangelift [ground
Caught his right hand and raifed him from the
Saying the while, " The fin has yet to'exift,
For which no ample pardon can be found
By Love that knows nor obftacle nor bound ;
Then be not faithlefs, but believe through all."
Chriftian recovered ftrength at that glad found
To bear, like Adam rifing from his fall,
The after-tafte of fin, the wormwood and the gall.

Evangelift proceeded thus, " Do thou
Give earneft heed to all that I fhall tell,
Because I am about to fhow thee now
The guilt of him who caufed thee to rebel,
And of that other fmooth-tongued infidel
To whom he fent thee ; now the former's name
Is Worldly Wifeman, and he earns it well,
Partly for that, though he the charge difclaim,
The doctrine which he loves from this world's wifdom came.

(" So always to the town Morality

He goes to church,) and partly it would seem,

Because he loves good works to deify,—

To save without a Saviour ;—in his scheme

Christ is superfluous, and faith a dream ;

And since his worldly mind is bias'd thus,

My righteous ways are vile in his esteem,

And his perversions of them dangerous ;

Now there are three main things thou should'st be sedulous

Most thoroughly to hate in this man's lies."

Poor Christian felt, alas, 'twas all too plain

Each lie had found its echo in the man !

Full of sad thought, he trembling turned again

To good Evangelist, and thus began,

" What think you Sir, is there yet any plan

By which I haply may regain the road

Whence, like a light-heeled fool erewhile I ran .

Shall I not now be bound to this my load

For ever, and be sent back to my old abode ?

" Alas that I gave heed to ill advice!
Can pardon yet be mine?" Evangelist
Thus answered, " Let these few last words suffice ;—
Thy sin is great and twofold, having missed
The right way wilfully, and dared persist
To keep the wrong; yet he who guards the door,
Goodwill by name, thy touch will not resist ;
But take good heed thou turn aside no more,
Lest God's re-kindled wrath burn hotter than before."

Then did the man address himself to trace
His footsteps o'er, and rose up grateful-hearted ;
One smile, one prayer, one fatherly embrace
Evangelist bestowed, and then they parted ;
So on the pilgrim hied, nor ever started
Out of the roadway, and all speech repressed ;
If travellers spoke, like some feared bird, he darted
On, on, and up the hill, where sunk to rest,
The new-born mist lay soft upon its parent breast.

The Wicket Gate and Goodwill.

AT laſt Goodwill approached with key in hand
To the'inner ſide, and aſked, what man drew nigh,
And whence he came, and what was his demand ;
Said Chriſtian, " A poor burdened ſinner I,
Who from the city of Deſtruction fly
To the Mount Zion, ſeeking ſo to be
Saved from the wrath to come ; I would apply
For entrance therefore, honored Sir, to thee,
Since I perceive thy gate bars the one path for me,"

*   *   *   *   *   *   *   *

" Why truly," anſwered Chriſtian, " I know not
What had befallen me, if Evangeliſt
Had but delayed his coming to the ſpot,
And failed to keep that melancholy tryſt
By God appointed, when He deigned to aſſiſt
A wretch who never elſe had hither come ;
Yes I, e'en I, unworthy ſo to have miſſed
That death, inſtead of lying cold and dumb,
Stand counting to my Lord love's yet uncounted ſum.

" And O, what favor is vouchfafed to me
In being thus redeemed from wrath and fear!"
" We anfwer all, however vile they be,
Or have been ; all have finned, but all are dear
To God," replied Goodwill, "and therefore here
Is none in anywife caft harfhly out.
Now through the clear and cloudlefs atmofphere,
Perufe the living map thus ftretched about,   [of doubt.
And melt with prayer's warm breath all lingering mifts

" Look onward, let that path be well furveyed
Which climbs towards heaven directly from this gate ;
By patriarchs, prophets, and apoftles made,
With Chrift's good help, it lies as true and ftraight
As fkill divine can meafure, therefore wait
And view it well, for 'tis thine only way ;"
Said Chriftian, " How do men difcriminate
The good old path, from byways which betray
The careful eye to rove, the cautious foot to ftray ?"

Anſwered Goodwill, " Though many ways abut
On this, yet all are crooked ones and wide ;
But the right way is ſtraight, as if 'twere cut
With God's unſwerving ploughſhare ; 'tis beſide
At times moſt narrow, be theſe marks thy guide."
Now in my dream I ſaw that Chriſtian prayed
For help to looſe that grievous burden, tied
Upon his back, where ſtill 'twas firmly laid,
Waiting the potent touch of more than mortal aid.

*   *   *   *   *   *   *   *

Cried the'other, " After travelling ſmoothly o'er
Some miles within the gate, thou draweſt near,
(If all go well,) the hoſpitable door
Of the Interpreter, and do not fear
To knock and wait until the maſter hear,
For in his ſtorehouſe joy and uſe are blended."
Chriſtian took leave of one made ever dear
In but a few ſhort hours, who then commended
The pilgrim to God's care, and ſo their meeting ended.

The Interpreter's House

SAID Chriſtian, "Gracious Sir, I here attend
By order of the gatekeeper Goodwill,
Who told me you would ſweetly condeſcend
With ſuch good things mine eye, heart, mind, to fill,
As ſhould not early die, but bloom in memory ſtill,"

"Come in," replied the Interpreter, "behold
Thoſe things of which thou ſpeak'ſt, and it ſhall be
To thine eternal profit ;" then he told
His man to bring a light, and preſently
He ſaid to Chriſtian, "Up, and follow me !"
And now he led him to an inner room,
Where, when a panel opened, they could ſee
A ſolemn portrait gazing through the gloom ;
And this the form of man that likeneſs ſeemed to aſſume ;

The raifed yet half-veiled eye looked glory fmitten,
The beft of books lay open in his hand,
Upon the lip the law of truth was written,
Its back to the earth, the figure feemed to ftand
Pleading with men, and lo, a circling band,
Like to a golden crown, o'er-hung the brow !
Then Chriftian faid, "Ah Sir, might I demand
The hiftory of him we gaze on now,
Before whofe feet my foul would almoft dare to bow !"

The Interpreter replied, " Thou feeft a man,
One of a thoufand ; who unites indeed,
Father and mother, nurfe and guardian,
In his own perfon, for the church's need ;
His eye in heaven, the book he loves to read,
The law of truth upon his opening lip,
His felf-forgetting gefture, bent to plead
With finful men, all this rare workmanfhip,
But faintly fhadows one whofe work effays to ftrip.

" Its film of darknefs from the natural eye ;
And this world placed behind him, is to fhow
How much he flights all pleafures born to die,
For love of Him who furely will beftow
Yon crown of glory fafhioned long ago,
Though hung in heaven until its owner's death.
Now this I fhowed thee firft, that thou might'ft know,
He who before us lives in all but breath,
Is that one man of whom the one Ordainer faith,

" That he is fully authorized to be
Thy guide through every danger of the way ;
And therefore hold him faft in memory,
For fear of thofe who tempt the flock to ftray,
Wolves in fheeps' clothing, hungering for their prey."

Passion and Patience

"UT as thou might'ft perceive wild Paffion fquander
All that he had, while yet life's day was young,
And feeft him now, a fhivering fuppliant yonder,
Hate at his heart, but prayer upon his tongue ;
So fhall the trembling hearts and hands be wrung
Of thofe who fix them both on earthly things,
When all fhall die round which their life had clung,
When drooping Fame fhall moult her eagle wings,
And Love's mute lips recoil like mufic's broken ftrings."

Then Chriftian faid, " Now know I that the younger
Is wifer of the two in many ways ;
Thrice happy! unto whom the fpirit's hunger
Is fure and certain pledge of harveft days ;
For whofe brow waits the feal of glory and praife
Infcribed with the unutterable name ;
While Paffion, like a boding meteor's blaze,
Or flafh of nitrous and fulphuric flame,
Dies almoft in the birth, a child of fin and fhame."

The unseen Renewer of the Sacred Fire

NOW in my dream the Interpreter next came
To Chriſtian ſolemnly, and led him thence
To watch a pure and ſolitary flame,
With one that ſtood thereby who ſtrove to quench the ſame;

Againſt a wall that fire continued burning,
Deſpite the water that he ever threw;
Higher and hotter, rain to vapour turning,
E'en from the moiſture freſher ſtrength it drew,
And quaffed it up as ſunbeams drink the dew;
Aſked Chriſtian, "What means this?" the other ſaid,
"This quenchleſs fire diſplays what grace can do
In man's regenerate heart, once cold and dead,
Now quick to love and truſt its former hate and dread.

" The one who ftrives to kill the living fire,
Is he who wreaks his hate to God, on man ;
But as thou feeft it hotter burn and higher,
Toil the infernal worker all he can,
The caufe thereof thou foon may'ft fully fcan ;"
Then fhowed he how behind the heated wall
There ftood that fire's perpetual Guardian,
Who, from a crufe like Zarephath's, let fall
Unquenchable fupplies, himfelf concealed from all.

" This, faid the Interpreter, " is God's Anointed,
Whofe hidden hands the facred fire maintain,
While that loft fpirit plies his tafk appointed,
Grows mad with baffled fury, clanks his chain,
And writhes to fee his develifh labour vain ;
The gracious form withdrawn from public fhow
Is Chrift within, fo figured, to explain
That men when tempted fee Him not, nor know
That in fuch drooping hearts fuch holy fire can glow."

The Man who Fought his Way into the Palace

 ALSO faw the Interpreter again
     Take hold of Chriftian by his willing hand,
     And lead him down a broad and pleafant plain,
Whereon a ftately palace feemed to ftand,
A glittering gem fet richly in the land,
Which dazzled while it charmed him ; and behold,
High on its battlemented top, a band
Of radiant champions clad in mail of gold,
'Neath royal banners flung from many a purple fold.

Then Chriftian fighed, "O might we enter thither!"
The Interpreter in filence led him on
Clofe to the gateway ; there thronged alfo hither
A wiftful company, but cowed and wan,
As fearful of the rifk to be o'ergone
In dread attempt to force an entrance there ;
And one fat near who, ever and anon,
Wrote in a book his name who fo fhould dare
To force the fteel-bound gate, to fcale the guarded ftair.

For Chriſtian ſaw that round the doorway ſtood
A band of men at arms in mail of proof,
Sworn to reſiſt each effort to make good
An entrance, and to ſlay or keep aloof
All who aſpired to tread that terraced roof;
And now he ſtood in deep and ſad amaze,
To ſee the pilgrims, for whoſe ſole behoof
That caſtle roſe, draw back before the rays
Of battleaxe and ſpear bright in the noonday blaze.

At laſt a warrior ſtern of eye and brow,
Towards the Recorder, with a ſtep sedate,
Approached; "Set down my name," he cried, and now
He lightly donned his helmet's ponderous weight,
Drew ſword, and ruſhed on thoſe that kept the gate,
Who met his ſtrokes with well nigh equal force,
But he unſcared and nerved with hope and hate,
Struck dead or wounded all who barred his courſe,
Himſelf baptized in blood from many a ghaſtly ſource,

And cut his way through all, and forward preffed
Into the palace ; whereupon a found,
(Sweet as the farewell kiffes of the Weft
Hufhing the woods at eve,) was breathed around
By thofe Immortals walking victory crowned,
Beyond the reach of change and death and fin :
And thus the towers melodioufly refound,
" Lord of the dauntlefs heart, come in, come in !
Eternal glory thou through God's free grace fhalt win."

And now the warrior having been arrayed
In like refplendent garments, Chriftian faid,
And fmilingly, " I need no teacher's aid
To fhow me how this riddle may be read ;
Now let me go or e'er the day be fped ;"
" Nay," cried the Interpreter, " awhile remain,
Until two further vifions, dark and dread,
Shall have been paffed before thee, then again
Thou may'ft purfue thy path along the cooler plain."

The Man in the Iron Cage

O taking Chriftian's trembling hand once more,
　　He led him to a dark and dreary room,
　　Where, fadder fight than any feen before,
Sat in an iron cage, a man, to whom
The outer darknefs of that living tomb,
(Which his dull downcaft eyes regarded not,)
Was funfhine, to the fpirit's inner gloom ;
His hands were clafped, thick-coming fighs, begot
By fin upon defpair, peopled that lonely spot.

Afked Chriftian, "What means this ?" the Interpreter
Said, "Afk the man and he fhall anfwer thee ;"
Then thus he fpoke to that poor prifoner,
"What art thou ?" almoft in foliloquy,
"I am what once I was not," murmured he ;
"What waft thou once ?" afked Chriftian, he replied,
"Ah, I was once like fome fair flowering tree,
And one whofe leafy dome rofe high and wide,
A fhelter to the flock, a glory and a pride.

" I once was bound for the celeftial city,
Or thought I was, and oft my heart beat faft
To hope that through its ample gate of pity,
I fhould obtain an entrance there at laft ;"
" Well but what art thou now ?" Chriftian aghaft
Inquired ; the other anfwered, " I am now
A wretch o'er whom the day of grace hath paffed,
Leaving perpetual night to witnefs how
I dint thefe maffive bars, thus with my blood-ftained brow."

"But how," afked awe-ftruck Chriftian, "cam'ft thou thus?"
The man replied, " I ceafed to watch and pray,
Unreined my lufts, became lefs rigorous
Towards my own faults and follies day by day.
Prefumed on God's long-fuffering delay,
Obfcured the heavenly light which fhines on all,
Grieved the bleft Spirit 'till He fled away,
Tempted the devil 'till he heard my call,
Provoked the Lord to wrath, who left me then to fall.

"And now my hardened heart can ne'er repent ;"
Then Chriſtian whiſpered to the interpreter,
" Is all the wealth of God's rich mercy ſpent ?
Has Love given o'er the work aſſigned to her ?"
Said the other, "Aſk him ;" " Doſt thou then aver,"
Cried he, "that hope hath fled away to die,
And left thee in deſpair's dark ſepulchre ?"
" I do," replied the man ; aſked Chriſtian, " Why ?
Is not the Son of God piteous exceedingly ?'

Anſwered the man, "O never more to me !
For I have crucified the Lord again,
Contemned His righteouſneſs and dignity,
Counted His cleanſing blood unholy and vain,
Done deſpite to His Spirit, and remain
Barred from all prayer, all promiſe, all endeavour ;
Nothing is left to loſe or to obtain ;
The fiend's triumphant voice rings wildly ever,
'Can ſuch a wretch be ſaved? No, never, never, never'!"

" What tempted thee to bring thyfelf to this ?"
Afked Chriftian, " For the luft, the gain, the pleafure
Of this loft world," faid he, " whofe tafte of blifs
Promifed me joy beyond all former meafure ;
But now each darling fin, each bofom treafure,
Creeps back upon my heart a quick-fanged fnake,
And faftens there to torture me at leifure ;"
Said Chriftian, " Canft thou not repent, and make
One laft appeal to Him who fuffered for man's fake ?"

" God hath denied to me the faving grace
Of true repentance," faid the man, " His word
Prefents no ground for hope in fuch a cafe,
Where e'en the pangs of hell are fcarce deferred ;
His changelefs fiat hath long fince interred
My life, my foul, in this untimely grave ;
Nor if the prifoner's ftifled moans were heard
Through earth and heaven, would they avail to fave ;
All angels and all men could never free that flave.

"And O, Eternity! eternity!
When I ſhall wake to thine unending day,
How ſhall I grapple with my miſery?"
Then did the Interpreter to Chriſtian ſay,
"Let the remembrance never fade away
Of this man's wretchedneſs, and ſo take heed;"
Said Chriſtian, "This is fearful, let me pray
For preſent help in every time of need,
And thus the cauſes ſhun which to ſuch iſſues lead.

The Day of Judgment

NOW is't not time for me to journey on ?"
   Cried the other " Tarry till I firſt have shown
   But one thing more, and then thou may'ſt be
So taking Chriſtian's hand within his own,   [gone ;
They reached a room, where pallid and alone,
A man was riſing from a troubled sleep,
Who, while his garments hurridly were thrown
Upon him, ſhook as though his fleſh did creep ;
Then Chriſtian aſked, "What cauſe hath power to pierce ſo
                                                   [deep ?"

The Interpreter then bade the man unfold
The reaſon of his fear, who thus complied ;
" Laſt night as I was wrapped in ſleep, behold !
The blackened ſky appearing to divide
In jagg'd and fiery chaſms, prophecied
The cloſely following thunder's deeptoned peal ;
I gaſped for terror, and methought I tried
To watch the rack which ſeemed to ſhake and reel,
As though the clouds were curſed with life to fear and feel.

"On which I heard a trumpet's piercing found,
And faw the Cloud-enthroned defcend from high,
Who, with in-numerable feraphs round,
Swept unimpeded through the flaming fky ;
And next I heard a mighty angel cry,
'Come up for judgment ye difperfëd dead,
Whether in earth, or fea, or fire, ye lie !'
The rocks were rent, the fhrinking ocean fled,
Earth's million mouths difgorged the flefh wherein fhe fed,

"And yielded up the univerfal man ;
Some were exceeding glad, their full eyes raifed,
With tears of grateful joy unbidden ran ;
But others rufhed, diftracted and amazed,
'Neath mountain crags, whence tremblingly they gazed.
Then did I fee the Cloud-enthroned draw nigh,
And ope the book of doom ; its letters blazed,
And fhot intelligence to every eye,
While on each human foul full flafhed the Deity.

" Yet 'twixt that soul, (how near and yet how far !)
And its Creator, rose a wall of flame,
As between judge and prisoner at the bar ;
I also heard a clarion voice proclaim
To those who with the cloud-throned Monarch came,
' Gather together all the tares, the chaff,
The stubble and the dust, and cast the same
Into the burning lake ;' with this, the half
Of being died, without one sigh or epitaph.

" For hell's unfathomed gulf had burst, and spread
Horribly wide before me, from which gushed
Smoke, fire, and moanings of the doubly dead ;
But soon as these sad echoes all were hushed,
The spirits who, with sweeping wings, had rushed
To warn the stars of God's approaching feet,
Proclaimed, while sad eyes glistened, pale cheeks
' Gather and garner all the precious wheat ;' [flushed,
With that, methought I saw the broad aerial street

" Grew populous with fouls that feemed to fly,
Each with its radiant angel guide affigned,
To everlafting blifs ; but I, but I,
How can I utter it ! was left behind.
Vainly I fought a fhelter then to find
From the 'eye of Him who fat upon the throne ;
My fins came alfo frefhly to my mind,
While wakened confcience groaned with hollow tone,
' Juft doom, which brings thy foul to meet its God alone !'

" At which I woke from fleep ;" Then Chriftian faid,
" What was it made you fo afraid of this ?"
The man replied, " Becaufe I thought with dread,
That the laft day had dawned on me, remifs
In preparation for it, hell's abyfs
Yawned at my feet burfting its broad confine ;
And what was worfe, while others rofe to blifs,
One foul was left, and that one foul was mine ;
My confcience pierced me fore, alfo the Judge divine

" Fixed, as I thought, on me His awful eye,
Unveiling all the terrors of its beams ;"
Then did the Interpreter to Chriftian cry,
" Haft thou confidered all thefe fights and dreams ?"
" Yes," anfwered he, " and well it me befeems
To walk in company with hope and fear ;"
Said the other, " Let remembrance of fuch themes
Be, as it were, a fpur to guide or cheer
Thy fpirit on its way, with me no longer near."

Then did the pilgrim gird himfelf to be
Prepared for travel, and the other cried,
" Good Chriftian ! may the Comforter with thee
Remain for ever as thy guard and guide,
Leading thee fafely through the defert wide,
Which every heaven-bound foul muft crofs, before
The city rifes looming in her pride ;"
So Chriftian left that hofpitable door,
And on the road he fang and viewed his journey o'er.

The Cross

THEN was he glad, and his expanding breast
Allowed the full-charged heart to throb its glee,
While thus he sang, "His labour gives me rest,
His bitter death brings happy life to me!"
Long, long, he gazed upon the hallowed tree,
For marvellous he deemed it, that the same,
Should so have instant power to set him free ;
He therefore looked, until his eyes became
Wet with a dew exhaled from wonder, love, and shame.

While thus he stood adoring, gazing, praying,
He saw three shining ones draw near, who cried,
"Peace be upon thee!" and the first one saying,
"Thy sins are all forgiven thee," stood aside ;
A change of raiment then the next supplied,
Stripping his rags ; and the last sealed his brow,
And gave a roll of promise, (which was tied
Close on his heart to bind him to his vow,)
The passport into heaven ; sang the glad pilgrim now,

A Hymn to Christ who died and rose again.

Formalist and Hypocrisy

                " BUT will it not be found,
O Friends! a daring trefpafs, and a crime
'Gainſt Him who knoweth whither we are bound,
And rules the place, if thus His dignity ye wound,

" By violating His revealed command ?"
They faid, " His tongue had little need to run
On their affairs, the cuſtom of the land
Confirming fully all which they had done :
And teſtimony contravened by none,
They could produce if called on, which would ſhow
That this ſhort way of their's had been begun
Ay, upwards of a thoufand years ago ;"
" But," anfwered Chriſtian then, " I fain would furely know

" If this your way of entrance could confront
A trial at the law ;" they told him, " How
This right of way, confirmed by ufe and wont
For twice five hundred years, would doubtlefs now,
(As all impartial jurifts muft allow,)
Be adjudged lawful ; and befides," faid they,
" We tread the highway, and what more doft thou ?
If we are only in, what matter pray
How firft we gained accefs ? are we not in the way

" As much as thou who entered through the gate,
Although we two came tumbling o'er the wall ?
Therefore wherein is this thy prefent ftate
Better than ours ?" faid Chriftian, " I take all
My fteps at God's command, you thief-like, crawl
Along the courfe your own rude fancies fteer ;
The Ruler of the way doth plainly call
Such pilgrims robbers, and I fear, I fear,
That at the journey's end your error will appear.

" You enter by yourfelves without His leave,
And by yourfelves your exit will be made
Without His mercy ;" this did they receive
With little anfwer, only on him laid
A charge to heed himfelf ; I then furveyed
Their further courfe, and each man went his way
Without much conference, fave that thofe two prayed
Chriftian to note, touching the law, that they
Were blamelefs as himfelf, and then went on to fay,

" We fee not how thou differeft from us,
But by the coat thou beareft on thy back,
Whofe comelinefs we need not now difcufs ;
'Twas doubtlefs given by one who faw thy lack
Of decent drefs, pitying thy wardrobe's wrack ;"
" The law," faid Chriftian, " will not ferve you, fince
You broke it when you entered on the track ;
As for my coat, 'twas given me by my Prince,
Who as you truly fay, His kindnefs to evince,

" Took off my filthy rags, and gave inftead,
This robe of righteoufnefs immaculate ;
And much it lightens every ftep I tread,
To know that when I reach the city's gate,
Its gracious Lord, will from His high eftate,
Remember one who wears the garb He gave
The day He ftripped me of the rags I hate ;
Moreover His near friend was bade to 'grave
A mark upon my brow, as feal that He could fave,

" The very day my grievious burden fell,
(Which mark of mine perchance you cannot fee ;)
And I am bold this further grace to tell,
That then a fealëd roll was given to me,
Its contents to be more than company
Throughout my travels ; I was alfo told
To fhow it fearleffly, when I fhould be
A fuppliant at heaven's gate, and then, behold,
The confcious fpirit gate would of itfelf unfold !

" Now all thefe things, my Friends, I doubt you lack,
And that because you paffed not through the door ;"
To this they deigned to give no anfwer back,
Only each looked at each, and laughed the more ;
Then I perceived that Chriftian kept before,
While all walked on ; nor did he fpeak again,
Save to himfelf a little, mufing o'er
His future of delight, his paft of pain :
He alfo often read while traverfing the plain

The roll the angel gave him, to renew
His fpirit's ftrength ; now did the pathway bring
The hill called Difficulty full in view,
And at its foot I faw a bubbling fpring :
Alfo two other ways, which iffuing
From the ftraight road turned toward the left and right ;
Nathlefs the narrow way did clofely cling
To the fteep hill ; then Chriftian drew frefh might
From the clear fount, and fang while climbing up the height.

The Hill Difficulty and Timorous and Mistrust

NOW half way up the hill fome fpreading trees,

    Whofe interlacing boughs an arbour made,

Showed that the gracious Lord who owns the hill,

Had planned this arbour of refrefhing fhade,

For weary travellers ; Chriftian firft ftood ftill,

Then fat within, (for fuch the Owner's will ;)

And here, when from his breaft the roll he drew

And read, it proved a balm for bygone ill ;

He alfo now began a frefh review

Of that white robe he wore fince firft the crofs he knew.

Thus pleafingly employed fome little fpace,

He dropped, from half-forgetfulnefs, to fleep,

Until the night drew near with ftealthy pace ;

Now while he flept, his hand forgot to keep

Hold of the roll ; at laft his flumber deep

Was broken by a man who came and faid,

" Go to the ant thou fluggard, watch yon heap

Garnered for winter ere the fummer fled ;"

With that did Chriftian foon ftart up and onward tread

Until his finewy ftrength and limbs robuft
Gained the hill top, where two men met him, one
Being named Timorous and one Miftruft ;
To whom faid Chriftian, " Wherefore do ye run
Thus backward o'er a way fo well begun ?"
Then Timorous replied, that being bound
Unto Mount Zion, they had fcorned to fhun
That difficult afcent, yet had they found
The further they had gone the more rifk thickened round ;

They therefore were returning down the fteep ;
" Yea," cried Miftruft, " for clofe at hand there lie,
(We know not whether waking or afleep,)
Two lions in the way, which terrify,
Then doubtlefs tear and flay the paffer by,"
Chriftian replied, " O Sirs, you make me fear,
Where fhall I turn in this extremity ?
If I go back to my own land from here,
That is prepared for fire, and my unbleft career

"Will end in death a few fhort years o'er-gone,
But if I only reach the heavenly gate,
I fhall be fafe, yes, I muft venture on."

The Missing Roll found

E went thus fadly on 'till rofe to view
That leafy arbour where he flept before,
At fight of which his tears gufhed forth anew,
So frefhly had it brought to mind once more
The fault that robbed him of the roll he bore ;
He therefore walked in forrow, thus bewailing,
"O wretched man as ever night clofed o'er!
Who flept until the fummer day was failing,
Then woke to fquander tears as fad as unavailing ;

" Who on the midſt of Difficulty's height
Could ſo indulge the fleſh, as to abuſe
With dreams of carnal eaſe and vain delight,
That ſolace which the Lord doth not refuſe
To fainting pilgrims whom brief reſt renews ;
And I have trod how many ſteps in vain !
So for their ſins did wandering Iſrael loſe
The readier way to reſt, condemned again
To tread the weary track of danger, toil, and pain.

" Thus am I made to take thoſe ſteps with ſorrow
Which ſhould ere now have led me nearer bliſs,
Nor can I be ſo far this time to-morrow
As now I might be, were it not for this ;
And I am forced to brave the precipice
Thrice over, which I need but once have ſcaled ;
Yea alſo I am like the road to miſs,
For now the waſted day has nearly failed ;
Alas, that luſt of eaſe ſo eaſily prevailed !"

Now he, by this, had reached the arbour, where
Awhile he weeping fat and deeply fighed ;
At laft, (in anfwer to forgotten prayer,)
While looking vacantly on earth, he fpied,
His miffing roll, which foon as he had eyed
Was feized and fafely gathered to his breaft,
With all the hafte that trembling joy fupplied ;
But who can tell what happy thoughts poffeffed
The heart which bore again its pledge of heavenly reft ?

He therefore kneeling thanked the Lord, whofe kindnefs
Throws light athwart the lids of weeping eyes;
Whofe hand can rend the veil of mortal blindnefs ;
Who holds the key of His own myfteries.
And now, while tears of joy and fweet furprife
Are mingled with the thickening dews of even
On Chriftian's grief-worn cheek, he leaves his fighs
With the arbour flowers, anticipates his heaven,
And feels his future fafe, with fuch a paft forgiven.

Christian's Approach and Introduction to the House Beautiful

HE called to mind the ſtory heard before,
  When Timorous and Miſtruſt their terror told,
  And how they quaked to hear the lions roar ;
He alſo thought, " Theſe beaſts are doubly bold
When night's dark curtains noiſeleſſly infold
The ſleeping earth, and were they now to paſs,
Their ſudden ſpring and their relentleſs hold
O how could I eſcape ? Alas, Alas,
How like the drifted ſnow my gathering woes amaſs!"

While thus he felt the grief-cloud thicken o'er him,
He raiſed his anxious eyes toward heaven, and lo !
A ſtately palace roſe on high before him ;
Its name was Beautiful, its caſement's glow
Sufficed his yet untrodden path to ſhow.
Then in my dream I ſaw him mend his pace,
Determined ſoon, if poſſible, to know
Whether the Owner of that goodly place
Would give the pilgrim reſt, would grant the wand'rer grace.

But foon the nature of the ground compelling
The road to narrow on each rugged fide,
About a furlong off the porter's dwelling,
He walked full warily, till he efpied
Two lions in the way, " Now, now," he cried,
" I fee the danger which drove back again
Miftruft and Timorous," (the beafts were tied,
Howbeit Chriftian could not fee their chain,)
Then was he fore afraid, and fcarcely could refrain

From turning ere he reached the palace gates,
Believing naught but death before him lay ;
But he whofe name is Watchful, and who waits
As porter at the lodge by night and day,
Saw him as though about to turn away,
And cried, " O Pilgrim ! is thy ftrength fo fmall ?
Fear not the lions, both are chained, for they
Are only there to try the faith of all,
Left thofe who walk by fight fhould reach my Mafter's hall.

" Keep thou but in the midſt of thy lone path,
And none ſhall harm thee."

"What houſe is this ?" aſked Chriſtian, " Sir, may I
Lodge but one night in ſuch a princely dwelling ?"
The porter anſwered, " He who rules on high,
Hath built this palace Beautiful, excelling
His other feats, thus lovingly compelling
His friends below to enter in and reſt ;
All He requires from ſuch, the truthful telling
Of their paſt travel and their future queſt."
Said Chriſtian, " I who now aſpire to be His gueſt

" Have from the city of Deſtruction come
And journey toward Mount Zion, but becauſe
The ſun hath ſet, am I thus troubleſome,
Seeking for reſt ;" the porter ſeemed to pauſe,
And aſked his name, " Sir, at the firſt it was
Graceleſs, but Chriſtian is my altered name ;
Of Japheth's race, (which our one Father draws
To ſojourn in the tents of Shem,) I came ;"
" But wherefore," cried the man, " our entertainment claim

" Thus later than the fun ?" faid Chriftian, " I
Had been here fooner, but that, fad to fay,
Within the arbour I flept heavily ;
And notwithftanding that illtimed delay,
Thou would'ft have feen me earlier in the day,
Had it not been that my deceitful fleep
Filched from my nervelefs hand this roll away,
Which lofs, not finding 'till I won the fteep,
What was there left to do but ftop, return, and weep?

" But God be thanked ! I found my miffing treafure,
And I am come at laft ;" the man replied,
" According to my holy Mafter's pleafure,
Some of His chofen friends who here abide
Muft I now fummon, they will foon decide
If thou may'ft pafs and I incur no blame ;"
A bell, with warning tongue for far and wide,
The porter rang, and with the found there came
That grave yet lovely maid whom men Difcretion name ;

Who asked why she was called ; answered the man,
" This pilgrim seeketh Zion's holy hill,
And from the city of Destruction ran,
What time he woke to do our Master's will ;
Benighted, weary, travel-worn, and chill,
He craved admission and repose 'till day ;
I told him I would summon those whose skill
Could test his truth and prove what he should say,
E'en as that rule directs which we are pledged to obey."

So then she asked him whence he was, and where
He meant to journey, and he told her straight ;
She also asked him how he entered there,
If o'er the wall or through the wicket gate ;
He told her ; next she asked him to relate
What he had seen and met with as he came ;
All which he told her ; and to terminate
Her lengthy questioning, she asked his name ;
" 'Tis Christian," he replied, " and I would urge my claim

" To lodge this night within your houfe, the rather,
Becaufe I deem it fafhioned with His aid,
Who though the Sovereign Lord, is ftill the Father
Of all the creatures that His love hath made :"
She fmiled a budding fmile, which feemed afraid
To bloom, left that might fhake the tender dew
From off the violet eyelid's spangled braid ;
After a paufe fhe gracefully withdrew,
And as fhe went, methought, the dark night darker grew.

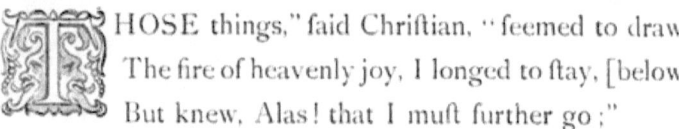

"THOSE things," faid Chriftian, "feemed to draw
The fire of heavenly joy, I longed to ftay, [below
But knew, Alas! that I muft further go;"
Afked Piety, "What faw you by the way?"
" It grew a little later in the day,"
Said Chriftian, "when I faw upon a height,
Wrapped in a bleeding robe of mortal clay,
One hanging on a crofs, and at the fight
My burden fell, and plunged into perpetual night.

" For you muft know that all my life I bore
A heavy load, but at the crofs it fell;
'Twas a ftrange thing! was ever man before
Unburdened by a hand invifible?
And while I gazed, like one beneath a fpell,
Three fhining ones in gracious fellowfhip,
Rofe fuddenly before me, one to tell
My fins were all forgiven me, one to ftrip
My pieced and worn-out garb, and in its ftead to equip

" My frefhened body with this flowing cloak :
But he who came the laft, thus figned my brow,
And gave me this fealed roll," as Chriftian fpoke.
He plucked it forth ; cried Piety, " But how
Saw you no more than you have faid e'en now ?
Is there naught elfe ?"   " The beft things have been told,"
Chriftian replied, " yet muft I needs avow
That I have ftill fome fecrets to unfold,
As namely, I defcried three men perverfely bold,

" Sloth, Simple, and Prefumption, fleeping lie
At fome fmall diftance off the narrow way,
With fhackles on their feet ; I ventured nigh
To roufe them, but how vainly, need I fay ?
I alfo faw on that eventful day,
Hypocrify and Formalift achieve
Their forceful entrance, fpurning all delay ;
Both foon were loft and doomed beyond reprieve,
Even as I forewarned, though they would not believe.

          *   *   *   *   *   *   *   *   *

"Such thoughts are grief, and could I rife to be
Sole sovereign o'er myfelf, I would at once decree

"Their ftrict and life-long exile from my breaft;
But though my aims are changed, my objects new,
Yet when I covet what I know is beft,
That which is worft is prefent;" "Is it true
Your arm at times is potent to fubdue
Such foes?" afked Prudence, "Yes," faid he, "though fcenes
Of conqueft are with me but fhort and few;"
"Can you," fhe afked, "remember by what means
You gain thefe golden hours when victory intervenes?"

"Yes, when I mufe upon the crofs I faw,"
Said Chriftian, "that will do it; and when I
This flowing robe without one fpeck or flaw
Contemplate, that will do it fpeedily;
When thought grows warm and flame-like fhoots on high,
Leaving this Prefent, that will do it well;
Or poring o'er this roll of prophecy
Will do it;" then faid Prudence, "Can you tell
Why thus you ftrive to fcale heaven's hard-won citidel?"

" Becauſe I long to ſee Him living there,
Who on the cruel croſs was ſhown me dead,"
Chriſtian replied ; " and in that purer air,
I hope to 'ſcape the clouds which overſpread
My judgment here below ; and there, 'tis ſaid,
Death's ſhadow never darkens happy faces ;
But I, by gratulating angels led,
And freed from all that fetters and debaſes,
With thoſe I loved on earth ſhall mingle ſoul embraces.

" In truth, my bark of life is ſwiftly ſailing
Toward Him who lighteneth all her load of pain ;
I grow more weary of my inward ailing ;
I long to live where death ſhall ceaſe to reign ;
And leaving ſuns that ſet and moons that wane,
To ſee that living Light which cannot die ;
To ſwell my Monarch's praiſe, to join His train,
Who " Holy, holy, holy," ever cry,
No ſin nor ſorrow more, a glorious company."

    *   *   *   *   *   *   *   *   *

Then Charity addreffed him thus, " Have you
A wife, or do you live a lonely man ?"
" I have a wife and four young children too,"
Said he ; " How could you leave them, when you ran
From your bad town ?" fhe afked ; he then began
To weep, and anfwered, " Willingly indeed
Would I have brought them with me, but who can
Plant in unwilling fouls the heavenly feed ?
All, all oppofed my courfe, none faw its vital need."

Then faid that maid fo brave yet gentle hearted,
" You fhould have talked to them, and tried to fhow
Their danger, ere you thus alone departed ;"
Chriftian replied, " Dear Lady, I did fo,
And I foretold our country's coming woe ;
But cold as thofe whofe funeral peal is knelled,
They counted me as one that mocked, although
Within thefe pleading eyes they all beheld
The grief of love unloved, of fympathy repelled."

" And did you pray to God that He would blefs
Your offered counfel ?" Charity inquired ;
Said Chriftian, " I may freely anfwer yes,
And that with zeal and conftancy untired,
For you may think how deeply I defired
The welfare of thofe fouls fo dear to me ;"
" But faid you, how your inward eye was fired
With that fwift-coming flame none elfe could fee,
That far-refracted flafh of God's artillery ?"

" Again and yet again I warned them all,"
Said Chriftian ; " they might alfo fee my fears,
In this fad face darkly prophetical,
Where clouds of forrow melted to the tears
Which hope's bright iris never fweetly cheers ;
Did they not alfo fee my trembling under
The dreadful judgment ringing in my ears ?
To them but as the uncertain diftant thunder,
When fkies are clear, and men fcarce deign to paufe or
                                        [wonder."

"What could they fay," afked fhe, "which might excufe
Their mad rejection of the proffered truth?"
Chriftian replied, " My wife was loth to lofe
This pleafant world, and the reft feemed in footh,
Prone to the foolifh vanities of youth ;
So what with one delufion and another,
They turned away, difcarding all felf-ruth ;
" But fome with ill example wholly fmother
The breath of good advice, did you thus act my Brother?"

Afked fhe ; he anfwered modeftly, " Although
I dare not much commend my way of life,
Full of miftakes and failures, (and I know
That he whofe lip profeffion is at ftrife
With daily conduct, wields the traitor knife
That ftabs at fweet Religion,) yet I may
Affert, that neither to my babes nor wife,
Did I give caufe, fo far as in me lay,
To doubt my truth, to fcorn the ftrait and narrow way;

" Yea for this very thing, they oft declared
That I was too precife, and blamed me ftill
When for their fakes, my felf-denial fpared
To do thofe things in which they faw no ill ;
And though my grief acquainted eyes may fill
With tears while faying it, the twofold chain
Which held them back from union with my will,
Was my defire to keep God's law from ftain,
Linked with that love to man which follows in its train."

＊   ＊   ＊   ＊   ＊   ＊   ＊   ＊

Now in my dream I faw that thus they fat
Together talking until fupper came ;
The board made ready, they were placed thereat,
And all the land could give, fupplied the fame
With food and drink ; but in their fpeech, the aim
Was ever toward the Lord who owns the hill,
As how and why he earned his earthly fame,
And wherefore he, of his own gracious will,
Had built that houfe for all who came its courts to fill.

And from fome words they dropped, I foon perceived
That fince the hour he firft drew mortal breath,
He had been bred to arms, and had achieved
Victory o'er him who had the power of death,
Though with apparent rifk and real fcath;
(O loved the more in that he bled for me!)
"For many an one of this true houfehold faith,
And I believe it," Chriftian cried, "that he
Did all to fave the land of his nativity,

("'Tis this which bathes his life in floods of glory,)
For which he forrowing lived and fuffering died."
Some alfo told this ftrange yet truthful ftory,
That fince the Saviour had been crucified,
They had both feen and heard Him; but befide,
They witneffed to the truth of every word,
When to their anxious thoughts He thus replied,
"My little ones! your ears have not yet heard
Thofe deeper tones of love whofe echo hell hath ftirred."

I heard them give this inftance of His love,
That He for them had caft His crown away,
And left His throne the higheft heavens above,—
Self-exiled God!—to affume a robe of clay,
And fave a world.   They alfo heard him fay,
He would not dwell alone on Zion's hill ;
And they affirmed that His reconquered fway,
And His augmented majefty, deigned ftill
The lowly foul to crown, the poor heart's void to fill.

They thus difcourfed far down the deepening night,
When, having wafted up to heaven a prayer,
That through the darknefs, God would be their light,
They went to reft ; the fpacious chamber where
The pilgrim lay, fhowed thoughtful love and care,
(Its name was Peace ;) with the firft glance of fire
From morning's eye, he heard a joyous air,
Trilled by the birds from the fweet fcented brier
Which 'neath his window grew, and Chriftian joined the
                                        [choir.

So in the wider dawn all met, and after
Some more difcourfe, they bade him wait a fpace,
Until from marble floor to oaken rafter,
They fhould have fhown the wonders of the place :
Firft in the Study, it behoved to trace
The meaning of the records of the paft,
Emblazoned with His deeds and high drawn race,
Who proved, when light upon the page was caft,
Child of the ancient days, albeit the Firft and Laft.

And next they culled from exploits numberlefs
Of His undaunted champions, how that they
Subdued revolted lands, wrought righteoufnefs,
Obtained God's promifes, kept ftill at bay
The famifhed lion roaring for his prey,
With life blood quenched the bigot's hell-brought light,
Efcaped the cruel fword upraifed to flay,
Grew ftrong in weaknefs, valorous in fight,
And turned with God's good help the alien hoft to flight.

From volumes treafured there they alfo learned
How willingly their Lord admitted all,
Yes all, to His free grace, though they had fpurned
His government, His perfon, and His call :
And in that world-remote and filent hall,
They fearched the records of illuftrious things,
Ancient or modern as their choice might fall,
Mingled with truths, on which the future flings
The fhadow and the dread of flow defcending wings.

Enrobed in darknefs moves the approaching Seer,
But lo! o'er-taking Time, he walks at laft,
In truth's full light, his voice rings loud and clear,
When once its deed has joined the lucid Paft ;
Then, then it awes as with a trumpet blaft,
The foes of God, and while appalling thefe,
It but confirms the faith of thofe who caft
The anchor of hope in heaven-reflected feas,
And wait to enter port with evening's favouring breeze.

          *   *   *   *   *   *   *   *   *

Then in my dream I ſaw that on the morrow
He roſe to travel, but they bade him ſtay
One night, that ſo the parting cup of ſorrow
Might ſeem to all leſs bitter, " For," ſaid they,
" In the clear morning we can well ſurvey,
From the hill-top, thoſe mountains which we call
Delectable, and though far far away,
The memory of their lovelineſs, o'er all
Thy intervening path ſhall like a ſunbeam fall :

" For they be nearer heaven than where we are :"
He therefore could not chooſe but ſtay ; ſo when
The hour had come for morning's dewy ſtar
To fade in brightneſs, as the life of men
Made holy, dies in light, they roſe again.
And walked around the terraced roof, and bade
Their gueſt look Southward, which he did, and then
He ſaw a fair and hilly country, clad
With fruits that made it rich and flowers that made it glad.

Vineyards and orchards, blossoms, streams, and fountains,
And wood-fringed meadows, a delightsome land ;
" How call ye those green fields, those purple mountains?"
The pilgrim cried, and thus the sister band
Made musical reply to his demand,
In tones which angels well might pause to hear,
" They be Immanuel's own, and those who stand
Upon them, deem the heavenly city near,
So flash its gates of gold throughout the ether clear,

" When looked upon with pure and loving eyes,
Through that perspective glass of faith, which He
Who owns the hills and valleys, still supplies
To all who join that shepherd company,
Guiding to pastures where the lilies be ;
For even as this place whereon we are,
The road throughout that happy land is free
To every pilgrim coming from afar ;
And paths which God makes wide who dares presume to bar ?"

          *   *   *   *   *   *   *   *   *

Now in my dream I faw that foon as they
Had found the lowly valley of their queft,
His good companions, ere they turned away,
With fmiles not unbedewed with tears, expreffed
Their fifter-love for the departing gueft
In more than words; they brake the hallowed bread
Which is Chrift's flefh; and fhared the firft and beft
Blood of the grape He gave, when bent to tread
The wineprefs all alone, dyeing His white robes red:

A clufter alfo from the vines which grow
Within the borders of the promifed land,
Brought by the meffengers of faith, to fhow
How rich its foil, its ripening air how bland;
Then Chriftian, having kiffed the offered hand
Of each kind hoftefs, made no longer ftay;
But fcarcely had he left that lovely band,
When up the vale, he faw to his difmay,
A foul fiend coming on to meet him in the way.

𝔄𝔭𝔬𝔩𝔩𝔶𝔬𝔫

"WHEREFORE from me, thy fovereign, haft thou fled?
     Did I not deem that thou might'ft yet give heed
     To my commands, I now would fmite thee dead,"
So fpoke the fiend; faid Chriftian, " Born indeed,
In your dominions, muft I toil and bleed
Through life about your bufinefs, when the wages
Of fin are death? a miferable meed
For tafks almoft as wretched; who engages
Never to mend his lot, nor mount life's higher ftages?

" Not I, who therefore grew folicitous
To leave your land;" then fpake the fiend again,
" No prince will lightly lofe his fubjects thus,
Nor will I thee; but fince thou doft complain
Of my rewards and tafks, only refrain
From this bold trefpafs on my power and ftate,
And here I promife thee to entertain
No one unkingly thought of fecret hate,
But all my land affords on all thy wants fhall wait."

" But I," faid Chriftian, "have engaged to ferve
Another and a nobler lord, for He
Is the great King of kings ; and fhall I fwerve
From my fealed promife, to return with thee ?"
The fiend replied, " Thou haft affuredly,
According to the old familiar phrafe,
Changed bad for worfe, yet do I daily fee
That thofe who crawl in thy new mafter's ways,
Soon flip his dog-leafh off, and 'fcape the lafh he fways.

" Returning unto me : and thus do thou,
So all fhall yet be well ;" faid Chriftian, " I
To him have pledged my faith, and made my vow
Of life-long fealty, therefore to comply
With mandates fuch as thine, would bring me nigh
To merit and to meet a traitor's end ;"
" Thou did'ft the fame to me in days gone by,"
Anfwered Apollyon, "yet I condefcend
To pardon all the paft, and hold thee as my friend,

" If only thou wilt now return with me
To fields through which joy's brimming river glides ;"
Then Chriftian anfwered, " What I promifed thee
Was in my nonage ; I account befides,
That He whofe royal banner henceforth guides
This arm in fight, this foot upon its way,
Is able to abfolve me, yea provides
A fpecial pardon for all fuch as lay
Their rebel weapons down, their paft be what it may.

" And to fpeak truth, I tell thee once for all
O thou Deftroyer! that I love His fway,
(Which thy falfe lip hath called tyrannical,)
His perfon, fervants, dwelling-place, and pay,
Better than thine ; ceafe then to bar the way,
And never tempt me more ; for I have ta'en
Earneft from Him, and here I ftand to fay
That what I am I ever will remain,
His fervant and not thine, who fpend'ft thy breath in vain."

" Confider yet once more," calmly replied
The artful fiend, " what fhadows wait to fall
Upon thy purposed path ; thou can'ft not hide
From me or from thyfelf, that well nigh all
Who thus refpond to thy new mafter's call,
Becaufe they wander from my ways and me
Meet an ill end ; earth's covering is too fmall
To wrap the bones of thofe we daily fee
Creep to that fhameful death whence I would refcue thee.

" And fince thou lov'ft his fervice more than mine,
Art thou fo dull of mind as not to know
That he, whom for mirth's fake, I call divine,
Has other work than thy affairs below
To heed and guide? methinks his arm is flow
To free his friends from my avenging hands :
But as for me, 'tis known that I beftow
Freedom on all who walk in my commands,
From him and his, as long as power or cunning ftands.

        *   *   *   *   *   *   *   *   *

" Thou waſt almoſt perſuaded to return
When the chained lions met thy timid gaze ;
And if ſhame be not dead, thy cheek muſt burn,
While I aſſert, that when thy works and ways
By thee are told, thy ſecret thirſt for praiſe
Is the mean motive, rather than God's glory ;"
" All this is true," ſaid Chriſtian, "and diſplays
Leſs than the half of life's unopened ſtory ;
And thy heart-piercing words, ſternly condemnatory.

" Although they be, I own are all too mild
To meet my caſe ; but He whom I obey
Has owned me, as a father owns the child,
Who home returning from an erring way,
Forſakes his follies ; let me alſo ſay,
That theſe infirmities and faults were mine,
Or ever I had left thy land, for they
Alas ! were then to me as luſcious wine ;
But I have wept them out with tears which Love divine

" Has taught to flow, and I am all forgiven ;"
Then burft Apollyon into furious rage,
Saying, " I hate this King of earth and heaven,
His laws and people, and I live to wage
Fierce war with him in every place and age ;
Know that I ftand to bar thy way, or fhed
Thy life-blood, down I throw my royal gage,
Accept it if thou dar'ft ;" then Chriftian faid,
" Beware of what you do, for I, proud fpirit, tread

The King's highway, the way of holinefs."

****

Then did the fiend, his long-fought time efpying,
Draw up to clofe with Chriftian, who fell prone,
Apollyon's mountain weight upon him lying ;
And with the dreadful fhock his fword was thrown
Out of his hand, worn to the gliftening bone ;
" Now am I fure of thee," Apollyon faid,
And preffed fo heavily, that one low moan
Seemed all that fevered Chriftian from the dead ;
Defpair drew near and paufed, Hope trembling, turned
[and fled.

But as the Lord would have it, while the foe
Was lifting high his arm, as if he meant
To make no fecond thruft or after blow,
Chriftian, by what the world calls accident,
Regained his fword, and thus he gave free vent
To the full tide of faith, " Rejoice no more
Againft me O mine enemy ! I bent
But like the bough, which when the guft is o'er
Rifes again," he thruft deeper than e'er before,

Forcing the fiend to rife as one who fprings
Pierced at the heart though whole in every limb ;
Then Chriftian faying, " Nay in all thefe things
We are made more than conquerors, through him
Who loved us," fmote a fecond time, his grim
And dreadful foe, who fpreading wing-like flames
Flew ftraightway forth to gain the diftant, dim,
And filent fhadow-land of thwarted aims ;
So Chriftian ftood alone to count his fcars and maims.

The Valley of the Shadow of Death

THE valley of the shadow of dread death
Christian must needs pafs through, because the
To the celestial City, traverseth   [way
Thofe leaden fields beneath their skies of gray ;
A lonely land ; one in the olden day,
Who knew it well, called it, " A defert place,
A land of pits and drought, a land where lay
Death's shadow, and whence none, but by God's grace,
Can e'er emerge to light, bearing no friendly trace

Of footfteps, and without a human dwelling ;"
Now here poor Christian's danger feemed to be
Greater than that which I have juft been telling,
Even as by the fequel you will fee.

*   *   *   *   *   *   *   *   *

" What faw you?" Chriftian afked, the ftrangers faid,
" The vale itfelf, which ftraight before us lay
In pitchy darknefs ftreaked with lurid red ;
There. by the momentary lightning's ray,
Loft fouls and fiends more deeply damned than they,
We trembling faw ; we alfo heard afar,
A difmal wail which never died away,
As from thofe hopelefs multitudes who are
Harneffed with iron chains to Satan's fiery car.

" And penfive captives to a milder woe,
Who fit with downcaft eyes, and weep and figh,
Wafted a found like breezes fobbing low ;
Clouds of confufion veiling the far fky,
Hung o'er that chafm ; and there with glaffy eye,
Death undifturbed fits brooding ; in a word,
It is a place given o'er to mifery,
And wild diforder ;" Chriftian undeterred,
Then faid, " I cannot yet by all that I have heard,

" Perceive but that my way to Zion's hill
Lies here ;" " Thine be it, 'tis not ours," they cried ;
And fo they parted, Chriftian walking ftill,
With fword unfheathed, and glancing reftlefs eyed,
Before, behind him, and on either fide,
For fear of frefh affaults.

      *   *   *   *   *   *   *   *

                .   . .   Then Chriftian faid.

" I pray thee grant deliverance to my foul ;"
Thus paffed he on a weary while, although
Still feemed thofe fiery waves impelled to roll
Toward him alone ; and rufhings to and fro,
And voices of a difembodied woe,
Made his ears tingle ; till there rofe before him,
The dread that by fome ftrange invifible foe
He fhould be torn in pieces, or that o'er him
Hell's hoft would tread, and none in heaven or earth de-
                              [plore him.

K

Sad echoes rolled and fiery billows gleamed,
While Chriftian travelled many miles in fear;
And coming to a byway, where he deemed
A cry of banded fiends fell on his ear,
As though they rufhed to meet him, he paufed here,
To ponder well what courfe he fhould purfue,
And the half-cherifhed thought, " Why perfevere
Againft fuch dreadful odds ?" at times fhot through
His troubled mind, but then the fweet fufpicion grew,

That he might foon be halfway through the vale ;
He alfo called to mind the ills o'ergone
Safely already, and that now to quail,
Might be more dangerous than to venture on ;
So he went forward, yet anon, anon,
Nearer and nearer came the hellifh crowd ;
But when the demons' breath fell hot upon
His fhrinking cheek, he ftopped and cried aloud,
" I walk with God the Lord, and with his ftrength endowed

" I bid defiance to ye all," they now
Gave back, and foon were hidden from his eyes ;
One thing I muft record, I noted how
Bewildered Chriftian failed to recognize
The found of his own voice, and in this wife
I watched the manner of the frefh affault ;
Over againft the fulph'rous flames which rife
Out of the burning pit's o'er-arching vault,
Even without his leave, or knowledge, or default,

There foftly crept behind him one of thofe
Whofe fole remaining hope of joy now lies
In dragging happier fouls down to their woes,
Whofe whifperingly fuggefted blafphemies
Too horrible to utter, feemed to rife
From the poor pilgrim's own delib'rate will ;
This new temptation in it's fubtle guife,
Struck deeper than all Chriftian's former ill ;
Him loved fo much before, yea loved fo deeply ftill,

To live to feel that he had thus blafphemed !
But Chriftian would have ftilled the horrid voice
Had it been his to rule ; he little deemed
It lay beyond the region of his choice :
How had it caufed his fad heart to rejoice,
Had he but known that ftopping his vexed ears
Againft the found caufed by that fiend-device,
Would have deftroyed it; hours that feemed like years
Dragged flowly by, (fo long a prefent grief appears.)

*   *   *   *   *   *   *   *

And now he knew how narrow was the way
Which he had paffed ; he alfo trembling faw
Loft fouls, and fiends more deeply damned than they,
Although far off, (becaufe they hold in awe
The rifing fun, and at his beams withdraw,)
Yet did he fee them plainly ; as 'tis faid,
" Deep things from darknefs, he who wields the law
Of day and night reveals, his wings widefpread,
Bring out from death's cold fhade the loft, the doubly dead."

More feared at night yet feen more clearly now,
Becaufe confpicuous in the eye of day,
Chriftian furveyed with fixed confid'rate brow,
The dangers of his folitary way ;
At which calm retrofpect of all that lay
O'erpaft and gone, the deep and hidden well
Of joy, uprifing 'gainft it's owner's fway,
Brimmed with quick tears which through their fluices fell ;
His lips were mute, his eyes fpoke love ineffable.

" Let there be light," faid Love in heaven, then flowed
The light on Chriftian from the victor fun ;
For note, that though the firft part of his road
Throughout the vale of death's dark fhade, was one
To 'appal the braveft, there remained undone
As hard a tafk, to wit, the paffage o'er
The fecond ; and his rifks already run
Were lefs, if poffible, than thofe before ;
For here were thickly fet by the infernal fower,

Snares, traps, and nets throughout the whole extent,
To the remoteſt verge of Chriſtian's ſight ;
And therewithal the ſurface ſo was rent
With holes and pits and ſhelvings, that had night
Still robed the earth in black, the pilgrim might
Have ſlipped a thouſand times ; but as I ſaid,
The victor ſun had ſcaled the bordering height ;
Then Chriſtian ſang, " His beams are round my head,
And by his light I walk, though dark the vale I tread."

And in this light he walked e'en to the cloſe
Of that dark vale.   Here alſo in my ſleep,
I ſaw the mangled limbs of ſome of thoſe
Who had been pilgrims once, a ghaſtly heap
Of aſhes, bones, and blood ; and while in deep
And anxious muſing what the cauſe might be,
I 'ſpied a cave a little up the ſteep,
In which two giants of one progeny,
Have dwelt in ſecret league from hoar antiquity ;

By the fell power and tyranny of whom,
The men whose sapless bones lay mould'ring there,
Were foully murdered ; but their open tomb
Christian passed through without much cause for fear ;
Whereat I wondered ; but that sway severe
Is, I have learned since then, o'er-mastered now ;
The elder has been dead for many a year ;
While th'other, though alive, compelled to bow
Beneath the weight of age, and scarred from foot to brow,

With wounds received when he was young and brave,
Is grown so stiff and feeble, as to do
But little more than sit within his cave,
Gnashing his teeth at pilgrims who pass through
This darkened vale, and ever vexed anew
Because he cannot reach them.   So, behold !
Christian went on his way, yet at the view
Of that grim man of sin, bent, palsied, old,
He knew not what to think, nor yet when plainly told,

By him whom grief and age had fafely chained,
" Ye ne'er will mend till more of you be burned ;"
But Chriſtian held his peace, and having gained
Some little confidence, went paſt, nor turned
A backward look at one who, beaſt-like, churned
The white foam of his rage with gory fang,
Who mercy from miffortune ne'er had learned,
Whofe thin ſhrill ſcream throughout the nations rang,
Troubler of church and world ; then joyful Chriſtian ſang,

" My gratitude vies with my wonder !
I have traverfed the darknefs at laſt,
The bolt-bearing lightning, the thunder,
The horrible pitfalls are paffed ;
I have threaded the fiend-haunted valley
O'erfpread with the ſhadow of death,
And now let me halt, while I rally
My courage, and gather my breath ;
Encompaffed about with temptation,
I ſlipped on the threfhold of hell,
But the arm of a prefent falvation
Around me was thrown as I fell."

Conbersation with Faithful

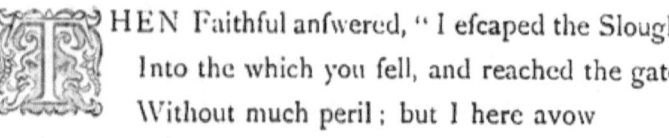HEN Faithful anfwered, " I efcaped the Slough
Into the which you fell, and reached the gate
Without much peril ; but I here avow
My fad difcov'ry that the fiend can bait
His fnare, with amiable and delicate,
As well as dark temptations, for I met,
(As Truth compels me blufhing to relate,)
That wanton dame who wanders to befet
And catch unwary youth in her wide filken net."

'Twas well that you efcaped her," Chriftian faid,
"She found chafte Jofeph in his prime of youth,
And he like you from her falfe beauty fled ;
Yet was that witch fo foully fair, in footh,
Almoft his death ; but for the fake of truth,
What were the arts fhe ufed ?" Faithful replied,
" You would not think how flattering and how fmooth,—
But that you have fome knowledge for your guide,—
Her honeyed words, diftilled from rofy lips that lied;

"And long fhe ftrove to tempt me from the way,
Still promifing all manner of content;"
"Not that," grave Chriftian hafted then to fay,
"Which waits upon a confcience innocent;"
"You fure might know," cried Faithful, "that I meant
Earthly and low delight;" faid the other then,
"O rare efcape! thank God for the event!
They who forfake Him, fall into her den,
Where luft and murder lurk to flay the fouls of men."

"Nay," anfwered Faithful, "I can fcarcely tell
Whether I wholly 'fcaped her wiles or no;"
"Alas, alas, my Brother, if you fell!"
Chriftian exclaimed; then Faithful faid, "Not fo,
For I remembered what was long ago
Writ with the finger of a fcribe of God,
'Her fteps take hold of hell,' and left her, though
I was compelled to fhut mine eyes, and trod
In a dim path awhile; I feared the avenging rod,

"Would fall upon me but for gazing on her ;
'O turn away mine eyes from vanity!'
I prayed, that I may dread to look upon her ;
But all fo clofely does deep hatred lie
To that bafe kind of loving, that as I
Departed thence, fhe curfed me and reviled ;"
"And did you not," afked Chriftian, with a figh,
"Meet foes who frowned, as well as foes who fmiled?"
Said Faithful, "When I reached the hills confufedly piled

"Called Difficulty, there a man I found
Preffed earthward with the weight of many years."

* * * * * * *

. . . . "This Mofes, man of men
Moft obdurate, exclaimed, 'All hope give o'er
Of mercy fhown by me,' then fmiting as before,

" He doubtlefs would have been my death, had not
One coming by enjoined him to forbear ;"
" What could he be who reached that lonely fpot
At fuch a time ?" afked Chriftian ; " Strangely fair,
Yet fad he looked, and I was unaware,
(For I had fainted,) who he was, at firft ;
But when his wounded hands and fide bent there
Above my wounds, the truth upon me burft,
I knew he was the Lord ; then foon as e'er I durft,

" Again I climbed the hill ;" " That man of wrath
Said Chriftian, " who o'ertook you, was the fame
Who fpareth no tranfgreffor, yea who hath
No touch of pity, Mofes is his name ;"
" Alas ! I know him well, 'twas he who came,
(For we," faid Faithful, " once before have met,)
Fraught with thofe threatenings of devouring flame,
Unto my houfe, which I could not forget,
Even while all around feemed deaf to danger yet."

Faithful meets Discontent and Shame

THEN Chriſtian ſaid to Faithful, "Pray you tell,
Met you no traveller through thoſe meadows
That valley of humility?"   "I well   [green,
Remember that I did," ſaid Faithful, "it befell,

"That one named Diſcontent beſet me there,
Who gladly would have turned my feet to go
Backward with him, for which his reaſons were,
Becauſe the vale was from its nature, low
And deſpicable, and that therefore, ſo
My waſted life in that mean ditch to hide,
Would diſoblige all thoſe I cared to know.
As Arrogancy, Self-conceit, and Pride,
With Glory-of-this-world, and many more beſide ;

" Who, he continued, would, and juftly, feel
Enraged, with fuch a headftrong fool as I,
(He prayed me to excufe his friendly zeal,)
Should feem to them, if ftill averfe to fly
From that deep valley of Humility."
Afked Chriftian, "Well, what anfwer did you make?"
" I told him," Faithful faid, "that though the tie
Of kindred was no eafy bond to break,
And thofe he named had long been loved for nature's fake,

" Yet fince I had a pilgrim come to be,
They had difowned me, and I partly them ;
That therefore they were now no more to me
Than if we could not claim one parent ftem ;
Touching this vale that he had dared contemn,
His judgment was too light to weigh its worth ;
Humility fhall wear the diadem
Of honour, while the haughty fpirit's mirth
Shall change to wail, it's lord laid grov'ling on the earth.

" Therefore, faid I, ftill be it mine to go
Along this lowly valley, honour-crowned
By wifdom, rather than to fink fo low,
As that my heaven-raifed forehead fhould be bound
With mud befpattered wreaths, which may be found
On every highway trampled by the throng ;"
Afked Chriftian, " Met you on that holy ground
With no one elfe ?"   " Yes, as I paffed along,"
Said Faithful, "Shame I met, but of all thofe among

"Whom I have mingled in my life-long walk,
He bears, I think, the moft ill-chofen name."

" ' And is not this,' " he afked, " 'a burning fhame ?' "
"And what reply," afked Chriftian, "did you make?"
" At firft," faid Faithful, " it was hard to frame
A fitting anfwer to the taunts he fpake ;
Yea, the hot tingling blood feemed to forfake
My heart, to flufh my face, Shame fhamed me fo :
I almoft thought I dared not undertake
To plead Religion's caufe 'gainft fuch a foe,
Until I called to mind thofe words faid long ago,

" 'The things efteemed by man, are with the Lord
Abomination ;' and I thought again,
Although this Shame, whofe word cuts like a fword,
Tells all too truly what is found in men ;
He cannot tell, for 'tis beyond his ken,
What may be found in God, by thofe who feek
In God's own words, pardon, ftrength, courage, when
Paft, prefent, future, as a chorus, fpeak
Of conflict to the ftrong, of terror to the weak.

" I alfo thought that at the day of doom,
The fwelling fpirits and the noble few
Whom Shame admired, will, rifing from the tomb,
(How changed and humbled by their paffage through !)
Not then be found my judges ; no, I knew
That life or death will fall to them and me,
According to the ftrict requirement due
Unto His law, whom every eye fhall fee,
Advocate, Witnefs, Judge, in triune Deity.

" Therefore, thought I, what God declares is beſt,
Is ſo, let all the men on all the earth
Deny it's excellence ; and for the reſt,
Seeing that Chriſt has deemed religion worth
Coming to die for ; that each tender birth
Of conſcience, and each infant fear of ſin,
With Him is precious ; that the very dearth
Of wordly wiſdom, in their ſouls who win
The heavenly, oft makes ſpace for the good ſeed within ;

" And that the pooreſt man who loveth Chriſt
Is richer than the richeſt in the world
Who hateth Him ; therefore, O Shame ! who lieſt
Moſt, when moſt ſeeming true ; who would'ſt have curled
Thy lip with ſcornful triumph, to have hurled
My ſoul to hell, thither return again ;
If my King's banner, borne by me, were furled
At thy ſolicitings, declare, how then
Could I endure His gaze ſearching all ſouls of men ?

M

" Should I be now afhamed of Him and His,
Would He not foon be found afhamed of me ?
So Shame was anfwered ; but indeed he is
A bold impoftor, I could fcarcely free
My path from his intrufive company ;
Yea, he would ftill be taunting me with one
Of the too many earthly ftains which be
On the faints' robe, kept white by nearly none :
But at the laft I faid that fpots upon the fun,

" Dimmed not his luftre ; that 'twas all in vain
To tempt me further in this bufinefs, feeing
The things he looked upon with moft difdain
I held moft glorious ; therefore our agreeing
Had come to be impoffible ; then freeing
My fnofteps from this Shame, I walked alone,
And felt at once the full delight of being
In no worfe company than e'en my own ;
So I began to fing in no defpondent tone."

" I am rejoiced, my Brother, that the ſnares
Of Shame," ſaid Chriſtian, "were thus 'ſcaped by thee ;
For as thou ſay'ſt, of all, I think he bears
The moſt ill-choſen name ; his face we ſee
When in the ſtreets, urging his hateful plea,
To make us feel aſhamed in open day ;
That is, aſhamed of goodneſs ; but if he
Were not himſelf moſt ſhameleſs, could he ſtay
So cloſely and ſo long, to dog us on our way ?"

   ※   ※   ※   ※   ※   ※   ※   ※   ※

Quoth Chriſtian, " You ſay well, but did you meet
With no one elſe when Shame at laſt withdrew ?"
Said Faithful, " No, not I, and light and heat
Were both vouchſafed me all that valley through,
And paſt the vale of death's cold ſhadow too,
For I had cheerful ſunſhine all the way ;"
Said Chriſtian gently, " It was well for you ;
It fared far otherwiſe with me, I may
Freely confeſs, that when Humiliation lay

A valley ſpread before my view, I fought
On entering it, a long and dreadful fight."

Conversation with Talkative

MOREOVER in my dream I faw that they
   Difcourfed at large on what the paft fupplied ;
   Now Faithful, as he chanced to look that way,
Obferved aloof, though walking at their fide,
One Talkative, (for here the path was wide,
Allowing room for all to walk abreaft ;)
The man was tall, and comelier when eyed
Far off than near ; whom Faithful thus addreffed.
' Whither away good Friend, are you, as we, in queft

" Of the celeftial city ?"   " Yes," quoth he ;
" 'Tis well," faid Faithful, " and I hope we may
Have your good company ;" " So let it be,
With all my heart," cried Talkative ; " Then pray
Let us together wend upon our way,"
Faithful rejoined, " nor in our walking, fmother
Young zeal with filence ;" " I may truly fay,"
Replied the man, " it pleafes me, my Brother,
To talk of holy things, with you or any other ;

"And glad indeed I am to meet with thofe
Who love fo good a work, for truth to fpeak,
There are but few, as you may well fuppofe,
Who thus, a way, tedious at times and bleak
Beguile ; moft pilgrims choofe in talk to feek
For things of little profit, which hath wrought
Some lofs to me, for though I am not weak
To lean, or much expecting to be taught,
Yet ftrongeft minds gain moft by interchange of thought."

"That is indeed a lofs to be deplored,
For what more fit to grace a human lip,
Than humble fpeech of heaven and heaven's Adored ?"
Faithful replied ; "I like your fellowfhip
Exceeding well, you let no topic flip
Out of your grafp without conviction's feal,"
Said Talkative, "and O! 'tis fweet to ftrip
The folds from myftery, and fo reveal
The hidden things of God, if we have hearts to feel

"Delight in what is new or wonderful;
As thus, if any love to dig in mines
Of unwrought treafure, or enjoy to cull
The field of wonders, miracles, and figns,
They find no book like God's, where joy combines
So fweetly with furprife;" "All this is true,"
Said Faithful, "but the fruit His hand enfhrines
Within the flower,—I mean what deeds enfue
After we fhut the book, fhould moft be held in view."

"I faid fo, for the light which converfe flings
On fcripture is moft precious; we by fpeech,"
Said Talkative, "explore unnumbered things;
By this, earth's vanity we learn and teach,
And bring heaven's truth down to our fpirit's reach;
Thus in the general, but to be exprefs,
The abfolute neceffity for each
Of the new birth, how poor and profitlefs
All works of man, the need of Chrift's own righteoufnefs.

" Or fuch like, by this means are taught ; I may
Alfo affert that thus by talk, we learn
How to repent, believe, endure, and pray,
And fo forth ; by this likewife we difcern
Promise and joy, when with our friends we turn
The gofpel page ; further, by this we know
How to refute falfe doctrine ; and we earn
The right to vindicate the truth, yea grow
Weak to inftruct the weak, yet ftrong to raife the low."

" All this is good, and glad am I to hear
Such things from you," cried Faithful ; " Ah ! the want
Of good difcourfe is one great caufe I fear."
Said the other, " why the number is fo fcant
Of thofe who know the need of faith, and pant
To feel a work of grace begun within ;
And why fo many, groffly ignorant,
Drag on in legal chains, a load of fin
Through life, for love not law his heaven for each muft
                                              [win."

" But by your leave, a knowledge fuch as this,"
Cried Faithful, "is the gift of God alone ;
And none that e'er hath been, fhall be, or is,
Earns it by fpeech or labour of his own ;"
" Which precious truth," faid Talkative, "is known
And prized by me, for every good we gain
Muft by God's Spirit doubtlefs firft be fown ;
All is of grace, not works ; I could maintain
This by a hundred texts, as forcible as plain."

" Well then," quoth Faithful, " what high thought fhall be
The prop round which our free difcourfe may twine ?"
" Whate'er you will," faid the'other, " I am free
To talk of earthly things or things divine,
Of law or gofpel, of the inner fhrine
Or outer court, of future or of paft,
Of foreign or domeftic, of the fign
Or of the fubftance, only may we caft
The light of truth o'er all, and profit at the laft."

And now did wondering Faithful quickly tread
Clofe up to Chriſtian, who this while had been
Walking alone, and foftly to him faid,
" A brave companion have we found I ween!
Surely in him may be diſtinctly feen
The pilgrim's model ;" at which Chriſtian fmiled,
But modeſtly, and anfwered, " He whofe mien
And talk you fo admire, has often wiled
By fcores, good men like you, whom he has juſt beguiled."

" Do you," afked Faithful, " know him then my Brother?"
" Yes, better than he knows himfelf," replied
Blunt Chriſtian ; " Pray what is he?" afked the other ;
" His name is Talkative, he ufed to abide,"
Quoth Chriſtian, " in our town, which fpreads fo wide
That therefore I fuppofe you know him not ;"
" Where lived he,—who his father?" Faithful cried ;
" Say-well of Prating row this fon begot,
Who is well known to all the neighbours round the fpot,

" As Talkative," faid Chriftian, " of that ftreet ;
And all defpite his deftly ordered tongue,
Search for a fummer's day, you fcarce will meet
A forrier rafcal or a founder lung ;"
Cried Faithful, " Well, I know that I am young
And inexperienced, but he feems to be
A richly gifted man ;" " That is, among
Thofe men who do not know him thoroughly,
For he is beft abroad, and fhould you chance to fee

" The man at home," faid Chriftian, " you would find
His daily life moft ugly ; what you fay
Touching his varied gifts, brings to my mind
A painting, which appears on clofe furvey,
Formlefs and falfe, but if we move away,
We learn that diftance is the friend of art,
Transforming blots to beauties ;" " Yet I may
Take leave to think," faid th'other, " that in part
You jeft, becaufe you fmile;" " No mirth fits at my heart,

" Although I fmile ; and God forbid that I,"
Said Chriftian, " fhould reap joy from others' crimes ;
Still lefs from ftooping down to vilify
Even God's enemies ; but there are times,
And this is one of them, when the fmooth chimes
Of modern courtefy are out of date ;
When what the weak call cruelty, fublimes
To the higheft mercy ; therefore though I hate
The cenfor's thanklefs tafk, I dare expatiate

" On this man's conduct ; he conforts with any ;
And as his voice with you demurely finks,
So is it pitched for the befotted many
Who throng the ale-bench, and the more he drinks,
The more he talks ; but whofoever thinks
To find the truth in this man's home or heart,
Finds only himfelf deceived ; her golden links
He melts and coins ; one feeming godly part
Alone he has, that tongue fo natural in its art."

Cried Faithful, " Say you fo! then how am I
Beguiled by this man's tongue ?" " Beguiled indeed,"
Chriftian replied, " but one who fcorned to lie
Thus wrote, ' They fay and do not ;' and we read,
' God's kingdom is not fhown in word or creed,
But in a living power ;' this Talkative
Speaks well of prayer, repentance, faith, the need
Of the new birth, but thefe words only give
The picture of that life he never means to live.

" For ftanding on his hearth, I learned to view
His life more clofely than a ftranger could ;
And what I fpeak of him I know is true :
His houfe is utterly devoid of good ;
Thence no prayer rifes, nor is underftood
Within thofe walls the meaning of contrition ;
Yea, the brute pilgrim of the field and wood,
Obeys God better, after it's condition,
Than he, who turns to bane the gift of free volition.

" He is to all who know him, known to be
Religion's very ſtain, reproach, and ſhame ;
Through him, her robe of ſpotleſs purity
Is counted vile, and few dare breathe her name ;
For thus un-numbered loathing lips proclaim
His life, ' A faint without, a fiend within ;'
His wretched family confirm the fame ; .
Such churliſh carriage and ſuch railing din,
Such domineering ſway o'er ſervants and o'er kin,

" Are ſuffered by thoſe helpleſs thralls of his,
That what to do, or how to look or ſpeak,
They never know ; the common whiſper is,
Amongſt the timid flock of poor and weak,
Driven to his miſ-named juſtice, ' Better ſeek
Fair dealing from a heathen than from him ;'
Moſt to be feared when fawning moſt, this ſleek
And ſmiling foe would ſmite them life and limb,
Were his the power, and they to croſs his gain or whim,

" Befides, he trains his fons to follow after
His crooked way ; and if in them he fees
The tender buds of confcience, with rude laughter,
With 'idiot,' 'madman,' and fuch words as thefe,
With fneers at ' foolifh cowardice,' from their knees
He fhames them ; nor will he affift to raife,—
Unlefs they firft obey his harfh decrees,—
Their worldly intereft, no, nor speak their praife
To any one who would ; fo wicked are his ways,

" That I, for my part, cannot think but he,
Alone has caufed the death of many fouls ;
And that if God prevent not, he will be
The death of many more ;" " Wife fpeech controls
Rafh judgment, and my Brother's fkill unrolls
The map of this man's life from early youth,"
Said Faithful, "and I know thefe rocks and fhoals
Are mentioned, not from malice, but in footh,
From Chriftian's love for me, for honour and for truth."

" Had I but known the man no more than you,
I might perhaps," faid Chriftian, " have been wiled
As you were ; yea, had this report been due
To thofe whofe lips and lives are fin-defiled
I fhould on hearing it have only fmiled,
And thought it flander ; (for fuch tales abound,
Where lie on lie is fhaped, and fmoothed, and piled,
To raife a fhelter whence the bad may wound
The fair fame of the good,) but Ah ! I grieving found,

" That all thefe things were proved againft this man,
With many more as grofs ; I alfo know
That good men are afhamed of him, they can
Nor friend nor brother call him, their cheeks glow
With fhame to think of him ;" " I feel I owe
The truth that words and deeds may dwell afunder,
Solely to you," faid Faithful, "may I grow
More careful to examine what lies under ;"
" They dwell apart indeed," faid Chriftian, "and no wonder,

" For they be diverfe as are body and foul ;
And as the body when the foul hath flown
Is dead, fo fpeech, if fpeech comprife the whole
Profeffion, is dead too ; by deeds alone
Can th' inner foul of piety be known ;
Thus is religion pure and undefiled,
Before our God and Father always fhown,—
In caring for the friendlefs orphan child ;
Soothing the widowed heart, till grief grow reconciled

" To life and God ; and ftriving to keep free
From this plague-fpotted world's infectious taint ;
This, Talkative is not aware of, he
Thinks that to hear and talk will make a faint,
And thus deceives his foul ; were he acquaint
With wifdom, fhe would fay to him that hearing,
Is but as feed time ; and fpeech, but as faint
And feeble proof of fruit indeed appearing
In heart and life ; and when the day that he is fearing,

" Shall dawn, be fure, whoe'er themfelves deceive,
Men fhall be judged according to their deeds ;
It will not then be afked, ' Did you believe ?'
But, ' Were you full-eared fheaves or worthlefs weeds,
Doers or talkers ?' and as each one pleads,
So is the doom.   The object of heaven's call,
Hath been compared to harveft, which time breeds
No thoughts but thoughts of ripened fruit in all ;
Not that I mean to'imply by what I have let fall,

" That aught can be accepted, which is not
Of faith."
        *   *   *   *   *   *   *   *   *
" What fhall I do ?" afked Faithful then, " Why go
To him," faid Chriftian, " fpeak with loving fkill
Upon religion's power, and afk to know,
(After he has approved it, as he will,)
Whether this living power indeed doth fill
His heart, houfe, converfation ;" Faithful here
Again ftepped forward, preffing on, until
He overtook the man, then cried, " What cheer ?
How is it now with you ?" " Well, thank you, but I fear

" That we have loft," faid th'other, " no fmall good,
We might have talked the whole way to this place ;"
" Well, if you pleafe, I, as no doubt I fhould,
Having been left by you to ftate a cafe,
Will now begin ; How is God's faving grace
Made known, when in man's evil heart it fprings ?"
Afked Faithful ; then faid Talkative, " I trace
Your queftion's aim, which is, the power of things ;
A bleffed theme, the thought expands my fpirit's wings.

" Hear then in brief my anfwer, to begin ;
Whene'er the grace of God hath touched a heart,
It caufeth there an outcry againft fin ;
And fecondly," " Nay, hold, and take one part"
Said Faithful, " of our fubject firft, nor ftart
Awry at the beginning ; you fhould fay,
Rather it caufeth there a galling fmart
Becaufe of fin ;" " What is the difference pray ?"
Afked Talkative furprifed, " Much difference every way,"

Said Faithful, "fome make outcry againft evil
From policy, but if we feel it's fmart,
And hate it, 'tis God's doing ; oft the Devil
Is chid with all the tricks of pulpit art,
By men who ferve him greedily in heart,
And houfe, and converfation.   The falfe wife
Of Potiphar, could act the outcry part
Of chaftity right well, yet was her life
Unholy, and her heart with evil paffions rife.

"Some againft fin make outcry, as the mother
Againft the infant on her knee doth cry,
Rating it well, and falling then to fmother
The querulous babe with kiffes ;" "Ah! I fpy,"
Cried Talkative, "that at the catch you lie ;"
"Not fo," faid Faithful, "for my fole defire
Is truth ; but what is your next fign, whereby
You prove that the one baptifm of fire
Hath cleanfed a human heart ?" faid th'other, "To acquire

"Clear infight into gofpel myfteries :"
Faithful replied, " This fign fhould have been firft,
But firft or laft, 'tis falfe ; the piercing eyes
Of man may fathom myftery, (fuch thirft
Hath he for knowledge,) with a foul accurfed ;
Yea, were it poffible for one of earth
To know the thoughts of God, and be well verfed
In heaven's decrees, he would be nothing worth,
Unlefs he alfo fhowed the fruits of heavenly birth.

"When Chrift inquires, ' Do ye know all thefe things ?'
And the difciples anfwer ' Yes,' He cries,
' Bleft are ye if ye do them ;' and thus brings
More bleffing to the good than to the wife,
To doing than to knowing ; He implies
That deep and varied knowledge may be ftill
Divorced from action ; which truth alfo lies
In words of His like thefe, ' His mafter's will
He knows, but does it not ;' a man may quaff his fill

"Of heavenly knowledge, yet not love the Lord ;
Therefore your fign is falfe ; and in my view,
To know, is but a ftate which doth afford
Pleafure to talking boafters, but to do,
Is that which pleafeth God ; yet is it true
That no heart void of knowledge can be good,
For without that 'tis naught ; therefore, in few,
There are two kinds of knowledge, one, that would
In fpeculation reft, the meer obferver's mood ;

"And one, that is united with the grace
Of faithful love ; and while this, makes a man
Strive to ferve God with all his heart, we trace
The former kind pervading the whole plan
Of the bare talker's life ; the Chriftian,
Unfatisfied without the other, prays,
'O ! give me underftanding, fo I can
Keep Thy pure law, yea, tread Thy holy ways,
With all my heart and ftrength all my remaining days.' "

Then Talkative replied, " I fee you lie
Again upon the catch, here is no ground
For edifying ;" " Well," faid Faithful, " I
Suggeft that, if you pleafe, you fhall propound
Another fign, whereby God's grace is found
By the fpectator, when it dwells in men ;"
" Not I," quoth Talkative, (who flightly frowned,)
" For we fhall ne'er agree ;" cried Faithful, " Then
If you will not, may I ?" and Talkative again

Anfwered, " O, you may ufe your liberty."

Evangelist forewarns the pilgrims of Vanity Fair

"WHEN, children, to that wicked town ye come,
Fierce foes will meet you, ruffian flaves of fin,
Who will ftrive hard to work your martyrdom.
And one or both of you muft die therein ;
But be you ' faithful unto death ' and win
'A crown of life,' the gift your King beftows ;
He that firft dies in pain, fhall firft begin
To live in joy, and thus efcape the woes
That lie in wait for him who haply further goes."

The Death of Faithful

THUS Faithful died ; as rofe that faithful foul
Elijah-like to the celeftial gate,
Sweet voices and eolian mufic ftole
To the 'rapt fenfe of him who yet muft wait,
And fee the end of this dark deed of hate,

Even to Chriftian's; yet the Lord, whofe fway
Is over all, was pleafed to moderate
The fury of the foe; and footh to fay,
The pilgrim for this time, efcaped and went his way.

Hopeful joins Christian.—The river of the water of life

HEN wound their way befide that tranquil river
Of God, which David knew, and called by John
The water of life; they praifed the gracious
Of this refrefhing boon, and journeyed on   [Giver
With great delight; all wearinefs was gone
At the firft tafte of that tranfparent wave,
And either fide the graffy banks upon,
Are trees whofe drooping fruit the waters lave,
Whofe wondrous leaves have power from threatened death
                                                   [to fave.

On each foft-floping bank, there grew the lily,
In fields the long year through as green as May ;
No need to fear the evening dew-damp chilly,
For midnight there was genial as mid-day ;
So wrapped in fweet and fafe repofe they lay.
Awhile they traverfed that delightfome land,
Which gave them all they needed on their way ;
Its ftream befide their path, its fruit at hand,
While airs breathed frefh from heaven their foreheads
                                        [gently fanned.

The Delectable mountains

AND now they reach the country where the mountains
Men call Delectable upheave toward heaven;
Gardens and vineyards, orchards, gushing fountains,
To scent, to taste, to sight, to touch, were given;
Each glittering morn, each many-tinted even,
They bathed in those pure waves of liquid light,
And freely eat the blooming clusters riven
From broad-leaved vines, the while far up the height
Were shepherds tending flocks, full in the travellers' sight;

Who therefore asked them, (as they rested, leaning
Upon their staves as weary pilgrims do,)
Who owned the fruitful hills thus intervening,
And whose the sheep that fed there; answer due,
Those friendly shepherds made, " It will, to you,
Be joy to learn this is Emmanuel's land;
The goodly place which ye are journeying to,
Is within sight; and sheep of His good hand
Are these for whom he died, though He all heaven command.

"So great His love divine and human pity ;"
Then thus the pilgrims asked the shepherd train,
"Is this the way to the celestial city ?
Is the road long, and is it steep or plain,
Dangerous or safe? and shall we reach again
Some hospitable place of rest and sleep ?"
They said, "The way through the great King's domain
Ye tread ; 'tis short or long, 'tis plain or steep,
According to your faith ; 'tis safe for those who keep

"The rules of Him who planned the King's highway,
But those who keep them not shall fall therein ;
And as to your last query, we may say,
That strangers reaching here we treat as kin ;
Which loving custom hath its origin,
In the strict charge of our dear country's Lord,
Who looks on all ungentleness as sin ;
Therefore fear not, our precious things here stored
Are yours, for they are His, Whose bounty be adored!"

At length the hour drew near to journey on,
(O change! of all thou only changeſt not;)
So ere the pilgrims ſhould indeed have gone.
The ſhepherds led them up to one clear ſpot
Commanding all the valley, nor forgot
To ſhow them through their glaſs of faith, at laſt,
The gate of that fair city where their lot
Should, as they hoped, eternally be caſt ;
But their hands ſhook in fear of what ſo late had paſſed

Before their eyes, nor could they hold the glaſs
Steadily, yet they thought they ſaw the gate ;
'Till a quick flaſh of heaven's glory, was
As darkneſs to them in their weak eſtate ;
But they remembered it, and learned to wait.

Help by the way

ONVOY is good, but it is better still
To afk the King Himfelf to guard our way ;
His prefence fo made David's bofom thrill
With joy in front of death, that he could fay,
'I fear no ill if Thou but with me ftay :'
And Mofes was for dying where he ftood,
Rather than journey for a fingle day,
Without the help and confcious neighbourhood
Of God, apart from Whom we are apart from good.

"And O my Brother! If He doth but go
With us along, what need to be afraid
Of tens of thoufands ? let the godlefs foe
Rife up againft us, fhould we feel difmayed,
Whofe weaknefs on Omnipotence is ftayed ?
Though I have fought, and through His help am living,
I cannot boaft of aught except His aid ;
And I fhould view my future with mifgiving,
Did not all victory dwell in trufting and receiving."

𝔄𝔱𝔥𝔢𝔦𝔰𝔱

ND foon they faw far off, as if to meet them,
A man approaching foftly and alone ;
So ere he could draw near enough to greet them,
Said Chriftian to his friend in warning tone,
"See one whom charity herfelf muft own
To be a faithlefs pilgrim, walking there,
His back toward Zion ;" Hopeful, cautious grown,
Anfwered, " I fee him, let us now beware,
Left he fhould alfo prove a flatterer and a fnare."

So he drew near and nearer, till at laft
They met ; his name was Atheift, " Though," he faid,
" This was but as a nickname on him caft
By bigots, and by dreamers fancy-fed ;
Howe'er," he added, " have ye fairly fped,
And whither are ye going ?" they replied,
" To the mount Zion ;" then he fhook his head,
And laughed fo loudly, that the mountain fide
Echoed the ugly found of fneering lips that lied.

They aſked, " What is the reaſon of your laughter ?"
" I laugh to ſee how ignorant ye are
Poor ſouls," ſaid Atheiſt, " in thus ſeeking after
A land, which like the mariſh meteor-ſtar,
Still flees before you, go ye e'er ſo far ;"
" Shall we not be received when we have run
Th' allotted courſe ?" aſked they ; " I know one bar
To your reception there, and only one,"
Said he, " that no ſuch land exiſts, when all is done.

" There's no ſuch place in all this world below ;"
" Yes, but there is above," quoth they ; " So, I,"
Said Atheiſt, " thought, or wherefore did I go
On pilgrimage ?   I heard the common cry
About this Zion, and ſet out to try
To reach it ; I have ſought it twenty years,
Yet can I find I draw no nigher, and why ?
Becauſe no city of this name appears
In any world but one,—the world of hopes and fears."

Cried they, "We have both heard there's fuch a place,
And do believe it;" Atheift faid again,
"Once I believed it too, or this fools'-chafe
I never had begun; but fince 'tis plain
That there is no fuch place, for I in vain
Have fought for it a longer time than you,
I fhall go back, efchewing future pain,
And feek my joy in thofe things which I threw
Behind me, lured by hope, falfe as my words are true."

Then Chriftian afked of Hopeful, "Is it fo,
Doth this man fpeak the truth?" and Hopeful faid,
"Take heed, one of the flatterers he; I know
The pain of having once been thus mifled;
What, no mount Zion! is then memory dead?
Did'ft thou not fee the gate of dazzling light,
When from the hills we viewed the landfcape fpread
Around? befides, we walk by faith not fight;
On, on, left wand'ring fteps frefh chaftifement invite.

"You fhould to me, not I to you have taught
Thofe words of truth, ' Learn, O my Son, to ceafe
To liften to the ill inftruction, fraught
With error, which forgets the way of peace ;'
Once more I fay, my Brother, we increafe
Peril by further parley ; O believe,
To thy limed foul's falvation and releafe !"
Then Chriftian fpoke, " O Hopeful, I perceive
Thy honefty of heart, and pr'ythee, do not grieve

"Or deem I held thy faith in real doubt,
I but confirmed it ; as for Atheift, true,
The lamp vouchfafed to guide him, is put out
By this world's god ; but as regards us two,
Walk we as in the light, in open view
Of every eye, as trufting pilgrims may ;"
Said Hopeful, " Brother, I rejoice anew,
In hope of the full glory of God this day :"
And fo they left the man, who laughing went his way.

Hopeful's account of his conversion

ASKED th' elder, "How was Chrift revealed to
"I did not fee Him with my bodily eyes," [you?"
Said Hopeful, "but within my fpirit view
Arofe the Form, now throned above the fkies,
Once crucified on earth ; and in this wife
It came ; one day I was exceeding fad,
More fad than e'er before, for in ftrange guife,
My dead fins paffed before me, darkly clad,
And larger than in life, like ghofts that drive men mad.

"And while I looked for nothing elfe but hell
For evermore, fuddenly, as I deemed,
I, even I, beheld the Invifible,
And the Lord looked on me from heaven ; He feemed
To fay to me alone, as His fmile beamed
Like life to my dead foul, ' Believe and live !'
I faid, "Ah Lord ! long, long have I efteemed
My fins too great and many to forgive ;"
' Sufficient is my grace, thou haft but to receive.

"And I do all the reft,' the Lord replied ;
I afked Him, 'what then is believing Lord ?'
And now I knew He fhowed that, when He cried,
'O hungry come, thirfty, believe My word,'—
Believing is but coming."

The land of Beulah, and the bridgeless river

NOW in my dream I faw that by this time
　　The pilgrims had o'erpaft th' Enchanted Ground;
　　And having gained the pure and genial clime
Of Beulah's pleafant land, and having found
That their way traverfed it, they looked around,
And chofe a place wherein to reft awhile ;
Yea, here they heard continually the found
Of cooing doves, and notes that might beguile
The road inlaid with flowers for many a velvet mile.

In that delightfome land 'tis always day ;
It ftands above the foul and murky air
Of death's dark valley, ftretching far away
Beyond the fartheft reach of grim Defpair ;
Neither could they fo much as fee from there
The towers of Doubting Caftle, for they ftood
In fight of that far-gleaming city, where
The pathway ceafed, and of it's brotherhood,
Some met them now with fmiles as elder children fhould.

For in this land the fhining ones do ufe
To make their common walk, becaufe it lies
Near unto heaven ; the bridegroom here renews
His contract with the Bride ; and bent his eyes,
Lighted with love that never wanes or dies,
Full on the pilgrims ; who found ample ftore
Of corn and wine, for bountiful fupplies
Of all which they had ever lacked before,
Were here laid up for thofe whofe toil was nearly o'er.

Here they heard voices from the City faying,
" Let Zion's forrowing daughter now be told,
He for whofe prefence thou haft long been praying,
And who is thy falvation, comes ; behold,
He gives and takes a meed more prized than gold
Or precious gem, He fows and reaps His love."
Nor were the people of the country cold
In greeting, but with gentleft fpeech enwove
Such words as thefe, " Ye faints, fought out, enrolled
⌈above !"

They felt while walking through this land of flowers,
A holier joy than they had ever found
In countries further from thofe happy towers
Circling the City whither they were bound ;
And drawing nearer to it's hallowed ground,
A yet more glorious view thereof they gained ;
'Twas bright with pearl and gem, and through it wound
Streets paved with gold ; fo faft the funbeams rained,
That way-worn Chriftian felt with over pleafure pained ;

And fo it was with Hopeful, wherefore here
Some little time they refted, while they poured
In every fwifter traveller's lift'ning ear,
The words, "Should you firft fee our rifen Lord,
(Whofe holy name be evermore adored,)
Tell Him we long to fee Him face to face."
But foon, with frefhened ftrength and fight reftored,
They walked with clearer aim and firmer pace,
Nearer and nearer yet their fouls' true dwelling place.

Paft orchards, vineyards, and frefh garden bowers,
Which opened on the road, they joyful fped ;
When lo! the Guardian of thofe fruits and flowers,
Stood in the path, to whom the pilgrims faid,
" Thefe goodly vineyards, and thefe gardens fpread
O'er all the land, whofe are they ?" he replied,
" They are the King's, who here delights to tread ;
Who alfo deigned to plant them, and provide
This folace for the few who have not fwerved afide."

Therefore the Gardener to the vineyards leading,
Bade them to tafte the clufters from the tree ;
Then to the royal bowers and walks proceeding,
He fhowed them where the King delights to be.
And here they flept in deep fecurity ;
Now in my dream I faw that for a fpace,
They, in their fleep, talked more continuoufly
Than e'er before ; and feeing in my face
Some wonder at the fame, the Guardian of the place

Said, " Wherefore do'ft thou marvel at the thing ?
Such is the nature of the vines that creep
Up thefe foft flopes, caufing the lips to fing
That touch them, yea although the fingers fleep,
So fweet the fruit which refting toilers reap ;"
Now when they woke, I faw that they addreffed
Themfelves to mount the city-girdled fteep ;
But as I faid, it ftood not all confeffed,
Becaufe its golden ftreets outfhone the dazzling Well

Of fummer's eve ; fo the bright flaſhes blazed,
That only through a glafs could they furvey
The glory fafely and with eyes undazed ;
Now I beheld that as they went their way,
Two men, whofe faces ſhone like fudden day,
And whofe ſtrange raiment flaſhed like Zion's gold,
Met them and aſked, " Whence come ye ?" to which they
Duly replied ; then aſked them to unfold
The ſtory of the way, and further to be told

Each difficulty, danger, comfort, pleafure,
They had experienced, and they told the men ;
Who faid, " You now have almoſt proved your meafure
Of pain, but two more obſtacles, and then
Ye are in the City."   Now methought, that when
The ſhining ones had ceafed, the pilgrims prayed
That they would ſtay the end ; and ne'er again
Did thofe two fpirits depart, yet anfwer made,
" You muſt attain your end by no external aid,

" But by your proper faith."   So in my dream,
I faw they went together 'till they ftood
In full fight of the gate ; but lo! a ftream
Rolled between them and it, a bridgelefs flood.
Exceeding fwift.   In meditative mood,
Yet troublous, bent the pilgrims o'er the river ;
But thofe who with them went to do them good,
Said, " Ye muft needs go through it, or ye never
Can reach the golden gates which open joy for ever."

" Is there no other way but paffing through ?"
They afked ; one of the men with pitying mien,
Said, " Yes, but none hath ever, faving two,
As namely, Enoch and Elijah, been
Allowed to tread that pathway fince, I ween,
This earth was born, nor fhall, 'till it's dirge found."
Then failed the pilgrims' hearts. (which might be feen
In Chriftian fpecially,) both looked around
Seeking a way to efcape, but no way could be found.

" And is the ftream in any chofen place
One depth ?" they afked ; the men replied, " Not fo,
Yet can we not affift you in that cafe,
For you fhall find it either ebb or flow.
As ye believe in Him to whom ye go,
Lord of the rebel waves and all befide ;"
They then prepared them for the ftream, but lo !
Chriftian on entering 'gan to fink, and cried
To Hopeful, that dear friend, " Beneath the whelming tide,

" I fink in the deep waters."
    *   *   *   *   *   *   *   *   *

With that a horror and thick cloud fell o'er
The dying Chriftian, who became as blind,
And could by no means fee what lay before ;
Yea, Reafon's helm, which guides the reftlefs mind,
He almoft loft, and with it caft behind
Remembrance and difcourfe of happier years ;
But all the words he ftill had power to find
Difcovered mental terror, and heart-fears
That his would be the death no hope of glory cheers.

Therefore his friend had much ado to keep,

His brother's head above the waters, yea,
Sometimes poor Chriſtian ſank beneath the tide :
Again a little while, and he would be
Raiſed up half dead ; when thus brave Hopeful tried
To comfort him, " Brother, for whom Chriſt died !
The gate, and men within it, I can ſee
Waiting to welcome us ;" but Chriſtian cried,
" 'Tis you, 'tis you they wait for, not for me !
You have been hopeful ſtill, through all our miſery."

" And ſurely ſo have you," replied the other ;
" Ah !" ſaid poor Chriſtian, " truly, if I were
At peace with God, He now would riſe, my Brother,
To help, but He hath brought me to the ſnare
Becauſe of all my ſins, and leaves me there ;"
Then anſwered Hopeful, " You have quite forgot
Thoſe warnings of the pſalmiſt which declare
Of the ungodly, ' In their death is not
One pang, their ſtrength is firm, and their's the envied lot,

" Free from the grief,' (which is a gift divine ;)
Thefe troubles and diftreffes you endure
In paffing through the river, are no fign
God has forfaken you ; be, rather, fure
That they are fent to try your faith, and lure
Your memory back to His great love of old ;
To prove that He is rich, though you are poor,
And full of need ;" Then in my dream, behold!
That Chriftian mufed awhile; whom Hopeful growing bold,

Thus fpoke to once again, " Be of good cheer,
Chrift Jefus makes thee whole." Then Chriftian cried.
With a loud voice, " Again I fee Him near,
Who tells me. ' When thou paffeft through the tide,
I will be with thee, and with Me befide
The river fhall not overflow thee.'" Then
They both took heart, and o'er the waters wide
The enemy was quiet, 'till thefe men
Had overpaft the ftream ; Chriftian felt ground, and when

He fo had done, the reft of that dark flood
Was eafy wading ; fo they gained at laft
The further bank, on which, behold ! there ftood
Waiting, their two bright comrades of the paft,
Who thus faluted them, " We have flown faft
To welcome you ; the cloud path have we trod
To minifter to you, whom mercy vaft
And marvellous, hath made the heirs of God."
Thus went they toward the gate, and feemed to fkim the fod.

The deſcription of the celeſtial City, and of the pilgrims' entrance there

THEN they who had been pilgrims aſked the ſpirits,
"And in the holy place what muſt we do?"
They anſwered, "There each happy ſoul inherits
The eaſe of all it's travail; there ſhall you
Have joy for all the grief you ever knew;
You there ſhall reap what you have ſown, and gather
Fruit of the prayers, the tears, the woes, gone through
For your King's ſake upon the way; yea rather,
Fruit of the love in you, ſown by the Eternal Father.

"And there ſhall you thoſe golden crowns put on
Prepared ere time began; you ſhall enjoy
Eternal viſion of the Holy One,
And 'ſee Him as He is;' ſtill your employ
Sweet praiſe and high thankſgiving, (ſounds that cloy
The ear of heaven never,) unto Him.
Your lovè of whom was mixed with much alloy
On earth, becauſe the eye of faith was dim.
There, with more cauſe to love than higheſt ſeraphim,

" You ſhall both ſee the Mighty One and live,
And hear Him with delight ; you ſhall again
Meet dear ones gone before you, and receive
Thoſe that ſhall follow after : not as men
Are clothed, to veil their ſhame, ſhall you be, when
You walk indued with majeſty and glory ;
Or on the obedient winds make up His train.
When, as was ſeen by prophet eyes before ye,
He comes with trumpet ſound to brighten earth's ſad ſtory.

" Riding the cloud ; there ſhall you with Him be ;
When He ſhall ſit upon the judgment throne,
You ſhall be near ; and when He ſhall decree
Sentence on all the wicked, let them own
The angelic name or human, not alone
Shall He adjudge them, you ſhall alſo ſhare
The high deliberation, becauſe none
Except His foes and yours ſhall tremble there.
Therefore when He returns to the earth He made ſo fair,

" You fhall come too with trumpet found and fong,
Yea, be for ever with Him."   Now while they
Were drawing toward the gate, behold, a throng
Of Zion's citizens, a fair array,
Came out to meet them ; unto whom 'gan fay
The pilgrims' two bright comrades of the paft.
" Thefe are the men who, in life's little day,
Have loved our Lord, and for His fake have caft
Earth's good behind their back, and we have travelled faft,

" At His command to fetch them, and thus far
Upon their journey are they joyful brought,
That they may mingle with the faints who are
Seeing their Saviour face to face."   Methought,
On this, the circumambient air was fraught,
Thus with the heavenly hoft's loud-voiced acclaim.
" Hail bleffëd fpirits, whom the Lamb hath fought
To grace His marriage fupper!" alfo came
To meet them at this time, thofe whom the angels name

As the King's trumpeters, to whom were given
Garbs white and fhining : who with greeting loud
Albeit melodious, made an echo in heaven ;
Ten thoufand welcomes from the tuneful crowd
Met Chriftian and his fellow, trumpets proud
And fhouting voices joined ; the joyful band,
With wings, as fwift as heavenly love, endowed,
Compaffed the pilgrims round on every hand ;
Some went before, and fome their momentary ftand

Took nearer earth, fome gleamed upon the right,
And others on the left, (as though it were
With melody and finging to invite,
And guide, and guard them through the upper air :)
So that to thofe who ftood beholding there,
The fight thereof was like all heaven defcending
To meet them ; therefore thus the ranfomed pair
And the angels paffed together ; and while wending,
Some, ever and anon, mufic with gefture blending.

Still fignified to Chriftian and his friend
Pleafed welcome to their blifsful company,
And joy to meet them at the journey's end ;
And now were thefe two men, as it might be.
In heaven before they came there, fuch a fea
Of mufic, with reiterated wave
Lulled their 'rapt fouls to deep ferenity,
And all fo fweet the fmiles the angels gave :
The City alfo here, bright contraft to the grave,

Rofe to their view, the while they thought they heard
All the bells there ring out, glad welcome telling :
But above all, how were their fpirits ftirred
With warm and joyful thoughts of ever dwelling
Therein, with fuch companions ; thoughts excelling
All that all tongues or pens could fpeak or write :
Thus to the gate they came, o'er which, compelling
Heedful regard, they faw in letters bright
And golden, " Bleft are they that, walking in the light,

" Do His commandments, and thereby can prove
Their title to the tree of life, their claim
To pafs the portals of eternal love."
Then in my dream I faw, that thofe two fame
Bright comrades of the paft, bade them to frame
A fummons at the portal ; which when done,
Some from above looked over ; Enoch came,
With Mofes and Elijah, to whom one
Of the bright fpirits faid, " From paft the furtheft fun,

" E'en from the city of Deftruction, thefe
Two pilgrims are come up, the love they have
Unto our country's King and His decrees,
Being the caufe ;" and then the pilgrims gave,
To thofe benignant patriarchs pleafed yet grave,
The feveral certificates they had
From the beginning, and had ftriven to fave
Through every peril ; thefe the warders bade
To lay before the King, heaven's meffengers were glad

To take them in ; which when the King had read,
He afked, " Where are they ?" and reply was made,
" They ftand without the gate ;" then the King faid,
" Open the gate, nor let them be afraid
To enter in, for they, by Mine own aid,
Have kept the truth, and I have kept them Mine :"
Now in my dream I faw that heaven obeyed,
For the gate opened at the Voice divine ;
And as the men went in, lo, glory feemed to fhine,

Not on, but from them, and their raiment grew
Luftrous and clear, as though divinely fair ;
Some met them bringing harps and chaplets due,
And gave them to the pilgrims, crowns to wear
For honour, harps the fweep of praife to bear.
Then in my dreaming ear I heard the bells
Ring loud for joy becaufe the men were there,
And it was faid, " Thus your glad welcome tells, —
'Enter ye now the joy which lives where Jefus dwells.' "

I alfo heard the men themfelves, to me
It feemed as though they fang in altered tone,
" All bleffing, honour, power, and glory be
Ever to Him who fitteth on the throne,
And to the Lamb."   Then I remained alone.
Now as the gate flew open to admit
The pilgrims, I looked in ; the whole place fhone
Dazzlingly, and its fkies were bright as it ;
'Twas paved with gold, and men on whofe brows feemed
                                        [to fit

Crowns, traverfed the great City, bearing palms
In lifted hands, or fweeping harps of gold
Inftinct with praife ; fome who had wings, fang pfalms
Together or alone ; and echo rolled,
What to a mortal ear may beft be told
As " Holy, holy, holy is the Lord :"
And after that I faw heaven's portal fold.
Then in my dream, fubmiffive I adored,
Yet wifhed myfelf with thofe o'er whom fuch glory poured.

www.ingramcontent.com/pod-product-compliance
Lightning Source LLC
Chambersburg PA
CBHW021135020726
47500CB00003B/1093